CLAUDE'S CONQUEST

Maura's Men Book 2

Stella Williams

Claude's Conquest

This is a work of fiction. Names, characters, places, and incidents either are the product of the author's imagination or are used fictitiously. Any resemblance to actual persons, living or dead, events, or locales is entirely coincidental.

Editing
Raw Book Editing
www.rawbookediting.com

Book Cover Design
GermanCreative on Fiverr

Publisher
Serpentine Creative LLC
www.serpentinecreative.com

Print ISBN: 978-1-953917-03-4
Ebook ISBN: 978-1-953917-04-1

Author's Note

This story touches on the topic of healing after physical abuse and mental abuse. Readers who are sensitve to these topics please be aware.

PROLOGUE

ROSEVILLE, TEXAS 1891

Claude smiled to himself as he exited the dark corner he'd been occupying with the beautiful young Miss—he'd forgotten her name already. Not that he could remember it anyway. The only thing interesting about her had been her ample bosom and lack of virtue. Claude lingered in the shadows only as long as he dared before rejoining the crowd in the ballroom.

He pasted on a neutral smirk and ran a quick hand through his sandy blond hair. He wasn't excited about returning to the droll, antiquated affair his mother put on every year. Some of the people in attendance still put on airs of being titled. He would much prefer spending his time with more worthwhile pursuits like coming up with new ways to expand his family's oil business. Claude might cultivate the reputation of a rake, but he was no idiot. His appetite for beautiful young women was only sustained by his family's continued wealth and standing in the community.

With his love of athletics, his physique was lean and muscled. He stood out against the soft, bookish types filling the room. It was a gift and a curse as far as he was concerned. While his build gave him a slight advantage in business dealings, it also made him a prime target for the husband seekers. For Claude, variety was the spice of life, and he had no intentions of settling down with anyone. It was only for the sake of his mother's health that he hadn't made his life plans known to anyone but a few close friends.

His friends were not where he had left them. They had probably left early as most of them had the same mindset as he did when it came to these events. A group of women huddled by the dance floor. Instead of the expected giggling and batting of eyelashes, they were focused on something that obviously was not to their liking. Their painted faces pinched in disgust.

Claude spotted his friend James amongst the group of men surrounding a beautiful but bordering matronly woman on the other side of the ballroom. She had every man's full attention as she spoke with them. He made a beeline for his friend. He wanted to talk to James about his latest business ideas and, as a bonus, save his friend from this obvious trap.

This woman had never been to any of his mother's parties before. Her escort had been an odd fellow as well. Not very talkative and he'd abandoned her for one of Claude's previous conquests as soon as the party had gotten underway. The woman was most likely some poor widow or old maid looking for a wealthy benefactor or, worse, a husband.

"Claude! I was wondering if you had left the party for good," James said, clasping his arm and pulling Claude into the group of men.

"No, just needed a little air."

The woman looked at Claude expectantly, her hand held out to him. He gave her a half-smile and a curt nod. If she thought he was going to kiss her gloved hand, she was going to be disappointed.

"Sorry for my friend's rudeness, Lady Maura. Let me

introduce Claude Morgan, son of our lovely hostess, Mrs. Lillian Morgan."

The woman smiled, but it didn't reach her eyes. He was uncharacteristically rude, but he was in no mood for games. He'd satisfied his hunger for the night and was ready to talk business. His mother would be appalled by his behavior, but he would deal with that later.

Claude turned his attention back to his friend. He grabbed James by the arm and dragged him away from the group. Claude could feel the spurned woman glaring fiery daggers at his back but felt confident her scorn would not last. The night was almost over, and he was sure that the men left standing in her little court would gladly entertain her.

"You didn't have to embarrass her like that," James exclaimed, as always, the perfect gentlemen.

"She's just passing through. It's unlikely I will ever see her again. Anyway, I wanted to discuss with you the latest gossip. There are rumors of a merger between our competitors."

"Can't I enjoy one party without the mundane conversation of business?" James smiled, shaking his head at Claude.

"It's hardly mundane. If the rumors are true, it could have a serious impact on the position of our company."

"The company or your ability to disregard women as you like? Don't think you were sneaky enough to go unnoticed, slipping away with Ursula Davenport. Your mother was brokering your marriage as soon as you stepped foot out of the ballroom with her."

"What? Her reputation is almost as bad as mine. There is no way my mother would force me to marry a loose woman. She is a lady of good standing and would only accept a daughter-in-law with the same."

James shook his head.

"Don't say you weren't warned. I've always told you your behavior would come back to haunt you one day. At least you know your wife won't be a total bore in the sack." James patted Claude on the back before leaving him to stew alone.

❋❋❋

Alexander made sure his presence was kept hidden in the shadows. Other than Maura's orders, his long hair and warrior's build didn't allow him to mingle. He wasn't exactly the party type, but Maura demanded he come as added security. From the open balcony, Alexander made brief eye contact with Felix. His fellow Vampire was wooing a young woman on the dance floor. The gesture was efficient yet straightforward to let Felix know Xander was still there, watching.

Tonight, watching was Alexander's only job, although he refused to be grateful to Maura for the slight reprieve. Alexander didn't know how Felix could do it, but he was glad he did. Watching as Felix led a beautiful young woman into a secluded corner, Alexander fought with his conscience. He might not be the one luring the women into Maura's lethal clutches. Still, he indeed wasn't doing anything to stop it either.

The girl was safe for a few more hours at least. Felix would convince the girl to "elope" with him. He'd come to her home later, and she would run away with him into the spider's web. By morning, they would all be off to the next town, the girl's body buried where it wouldn't be found for years.

A familiar twinge of guilt tugged at Alexander.

My dear Rachel, I am sorry.

Ever since Rachel, he hadn't been very good at that

4

particular task. He had seen her face in every girl he had attempted to lure. His guilt had eaten him alive, so more often than not, the women had managed to escape before he could get them to Maura. He could have easily stopped them, but that was too much for Alexander to bear. Maura had been furious at first but had eventually shown him a bit of mercy.

He had hoped that meant that Maura would kill him and end his suffering. It was only the worst luck that Maura had other uses for him in and out of her bedchamber. She'd killed him once before, if only she had left him that way. Maura had coveted his strength. Felix was better with women initially, but he didn't suit Maura's more basic urges. He was too weak to handle her barbaric idea of lovemaking. That job now fell to Alexander almost exclusively. If only there were a way to end it all.

He forced his gaze away from Felix and his prey. Instead, he skimmed the crowd for Maura. The harpy was holding court with a group of young men eager to court her attention. Maura was in her element, soaking in their adulation. Still, Alexander noticed her eyes kept shifting off to another part of the room. He followed her gaze, finally landing on the object of her fascination.

The man was tall and athletically built. He was not a warrior, but he didn't seem to fit in with the rest of the dandies floating around the room. His eyes seemed to catch Maura looking in his direction. The man smirked before crossing the room towards the double doors that led to the gardens, leaving his companion looking exasperated. Alexander had a bad feeling that tonight was going to be more challenging than he had expected. His suspicions were confirmed a few moments later when he saw Maura follow the man out.

❋❋❋

Claude was furious both with his friend and himself. He doubted he would be able to return to the party tonight. His mood was so black, even the air in the garden seemed off. He had always prided himself on being one step ahead of the husband-hungry women and their mothers. Now that he looked back on the earlier events, he should have seen that it had all been too easy. It had been a trap, and he had walked right into it.

"How dare you," a female voice said from behind Claude.

It wasn't one he recognized, but he turned anyway. He wasn't accustomed to open admonishment by anyone other than his own mother. He smirked as he saw the old maid from earlier. Her face twisted with rage that added even more age to her features. He wondered exactly how old she truly was. The soft lighting of the ballroom had given her skin a youthful glow, but out in the gardens, with only the light of the moon casting shadows on every wrinkle, he saw the true horror she was.

"I'm not in the mood to deal with the hurt feelings of an angry old maid. Why don't you return to your desperate suitors in a light more forgiving to someone of your advanced years?" Claude suggested before turning back down the path he had come.

Claude heard an inhuman growl before he was grabbed tightly from behind. His whole body went on the defense as he came face to face with pure evil. He stared down into soulless black eyes as the woman held him off the ground by his neck. As if she sensed his fear, the creature smiled, revealing a pair of long sharp canines that had Claude ready to piss his pants.

"You will learn that I am not a woman to disrespect,"

she ground out before sinking her teeth into the crook of his neck.

❀❀❀

Alexander cursed silently as he took in the carnage at Maura's feet. The man's neck looked nearly severed from the torso. He paused a moment to make sure no one was around as he picked up the body. Alexander was good at being stealthy, but from the way blood was seeping into his clothes, he knew he would have to back-track to cover up the trail of blood. Maura's blood was already beginning to mend the gaping neck wound.

Another man had fallen prey to Maura. Alexander wasn't surprised that Maura had escaped sullying her clothes with her latest carnage. He knew she had years of practice and maybe even some mystical help. The only trace of her evil was a small ring of blood around her mouth. The sight of her in her element, enjoying the rush she undoubtedly felt from a fresh kill, was sickening. Still, Alexander knew better than to show any signs of disgust. That had been this man's downfall, after all.

"Take Claude back to the estate," Maura ordered after licking her mouth clean. She stalked off back toward the party.

As much as Alexander hated the MacDonald Estate, it was better than staying with Maura. Even if only for a day, Alexander would relish the solitude without her overbearing presence. The only problem was the long journey back to Scotland. He would have to use that time to train Maura's new pet.

Alexander headed away from the lights of the party. He would leave the carriage for Maura and use his inhuman speed to avoid detection. Maura's blood was powerful. It was only a matter of minutes before the limp body in his arms began to change. He hoped to get to the house they were staying in before the man came back to life.

"Welcome to hell," Alexander greeted Claude when he came to.

"What happened, and who are you?" The man's voice was raspy and weak.

"Alexander. You pissed off the wrong she-devil. You are now the property of Maura."

The man tried to sit up but fell back against the bed.

"Maura? You mean the crazy old hag that cornered me in the garden?"

"I wouldn't say that to her face, but yes, the one and only."

"What the hell did she do to me? The crazy old bat had to poison me somehow." He reached a hand up to his neck and grimaced with pain. He paled further at the sight of blood on his fingers.

"You're right. It was poison. With her demon venom, she poisoned your soul. You are no longer of the living. I'd explain more, but there will be plenty of time on our voyage," Alexander said, tossing Claude clean clothing.

His wound hand already stopped bleeding; the change having already sped up the healing process. They weren't as lovely as his party clothes and would probably be too loose. Seeing as the ones he was currently wearing were now covered in blood, the man had no choice but to change.

"What voyage?"

"I'll explain everything I know, but for now, change out of those clothes."

"Well, are you just going to stand there and watch?" Claude glared at him.

Alexander glared back before leaving him alone to

change. The last thing Alexander wanted was to babysit a new Vampire. It wasn't like he had a choice, however. If anyone was going to show him the ropes, it was better that Alexander did it than Felix. No matter how charming Felix acted, it was his lack of empathy and conscience that bothered Alexander to no end. At least this way, Alexander might have an ally in the den of snakes he had found himself.

Alexander had his work cut out for him. Even now, he knew the newcomer was forming a plan as he pretended to accept everything. Alexander had been the same initially, but the man who had trained him had been a lot rougher than he planned to be.

Being a new Vampire, Claude was defenseless against Alexander's superior senses. The heightened hearing allowed him to hear the light rustling of the hay stuffed mattress as the man moved around, then the slight creak of the loose floorboard by the open window. It was those senses and Alexander's own experience that allowed him to know precisely what Claude was doing.

Just as Claude was about to make his move, Alexander quickly shoved the door open, startling Claude from his perch in the window. His grip slipped, and he almost toppled out of the open window, but Alexander was too quick. Claude was grabbed from mid-fall and deposited back in the dreary room where he was being held.

"Nice try, but just so you have no further misunderstanding of your situation, you can't go back to your old life. It would mean the death of everyone you hold dear. I am faster and smarter than you will ever be. You need my help if you are going to survive the hell that is in store for you."

Claude seemed to realize the dire situation he was in. Still, instead of cowering and showing fear, he plastered on an arrogant smile. Maybe training him wouldn't be so rough after all. While his arrogance was what got him killed in the first place, it would also be his only salvation in dealing with Maura.

❋❋❋

DRAWN

Gretchen "Liz" Jones leaned forward in her seat as the photo of a stone fortress came upon the massive projection screen at the front of the class. "And now for our guest lecturer, Dr. Felix Aiken." Professor Magnus motioned to a man who had been standing off to the side. Gretchen hadn't noticed him before Magnus gestured towards him. He was tall and surprisingly youthful for his age. He'd been researching the MacDonald Estate for nearly fifteen years, and yet he barely looked a day over 25.

"Who's the hottie?" Hailey stopped chatting with Gina finally to pay attention to something other than her latest shopping adventure.

Dr. Aiken began his speech, and Hailey lost interest almost immediately. She wasn't the academic type, and to be honest, neither was Gretchen, but something about him had her undivided attention. It was Dr. Aiken who had introduced her to the wonder that was MacDonald Estate. She was mesmerized by the photos he scrolled through large stone structures, a fairytale garden, and the creepiest looking woodline she had ever seen. Gretchen took notes on everything while her friends mocked the lecture. Their childish questions irked her very soul. Stupid questions like, "Where did Ronald store his wigs?" and "Was Hamburglar a welcome guest, or did he just break-in during parties?"

"Can you guys shut up! I'm actually trying to hear what he says," Gretchen snapped at Gina and Hailey.

Both girls looked at her like she had just grown a pig head.

"You know being a bitch is never a good look," Hailey said before continuing her obnoxious conversation with Gina.

Any other time Gretchen probably would have joined in on the fun, but she had just received a significant wake-up call the night before. Her two best friends had yet to ask about her mysterious disappearance during the frat party. If anything, they were upset with her for taking off with Justin Finch. Justin had always been an aggressive flirt, but she had never taken him seriously. That night he had force-fed her drinks and laced innuendo into every sentence of their conversation. When she'd been drunk out of her mind, he dragged her into a private room.

Gretchen didn't want to think about what would have happened if one of Justin's frat brothers hadn't stumbled in. That, however, had only fueled the rumor mill. By the next morning, Justin was "the man" for getting into her pants, and Gretchen, or "Liz" as her friends called her, Liz was a whore for sleeping with her best friend's man. Gretchen had thought about trying to defend her reputation, but he was Justin Finch. The quintessential charmer, every girl on campus wanted to be with him. No one would believe that he had tried to force himself on her when he had his choice of willing females.

To avoid the chaos in her brain, she focused all her attention on the guest lecture. Of course, she noticed how Dr. Aiken glossed over the stories about missing young women and a mysterious head of household that never seemed to age, but she couldn't really blame him.

He probably wasn't much for unsubstantiated gossip. Something Gretchen was suddenly tired of as well. Almost as if she were drawn to him, she hung back after the lecture to speak with him.

"Seriously, Liz, first you go after Justin, and now you're fawning over some old fart," Gina sneered.

Gretchen frowned. She had told Gina and Hailey to go on without her.

"You have no fucking clue what you're talking about." She pushed past them and headed towards Dr. Aiken.

Dr. Aiken smiled pleasantly at her, and she took a deep breath. She had no clue what she was going to talk to him about. He'd been very thorough in his lecture. She stopped just short of the podium where he stood and opened her mouth to start some small talk, only to end up spilling the whole sordid tale of the night before. He'd listened quietly, and even though he barely said a word, Gretchen felt at ease for once in the past 24 hours. In the end, they had exchanged contact information. He had encouraged her to apply for an internship with his department in Scotland.

✹✹✹

Felix hadn't been able to keep his focus on his presentation. Not because of the imbecilic questions from his less than an attentive audience, it was an overwhelming sadness emanating from one student in particular that had him so distracted. She sat with the worst of the offenders. Still, she was quiet and seemed the most interested in what he was talking about, except maybe the professor who invited him to come. Despite himself, Felix found himself drawing the young lady to him.

It was a bad habit from his time under Maura's

thumb. He could hardly pass a woman in distress, especially a beautiful young woman. She was average in height and build. There weren't many curves to be seen in her slightly baggy attire. Still, judging by the bleach blonde hair cascading over her shoulders and dramatic smoky-eyed makeup that enhanced the gray of her eyes, this wasn't her usual mode of dress. Other than her clothing and mood, everything about her screamed 'I'm a party girl, come play with me.' She reminded Felix of a time long ago, a time he so desperately wanted to forget.

Felix tried not to frown as he noticed Maura's curiosity in the man entering the room. This could hardly be a good thing. This whole night was only to cultivate some fresh blood for Maura's latest beauty binge, not to add another toy soldier to her collection. Felix turned his attention back to the charming young woman in front of him. Many years had passed, but it seemed the only thing that had changed was fashion. This woman was so enticed by the thought of a future with him it was almost too easy to convince her to slip away with him later. Felix desperately wanted to have a conscience as he began to lead the girl away from the party. Still, it had been a long time since Felix had felt human enough to have that kind of emotion.

As the girl got closer, her emotional turmoil ripped him out of his self-loathing. Why the woman had coaxed the memory of his first encounter with Claude, he had no idea, maybe because it was the first time that Felix had ever questioned Maura's motives. Felix felt the familiar stirrings within himself, the lust for blood mixed with the need to possess. It wasn't until they were face to face that Felix knew that this was something different. The look in her eyes was too eerily familiar for him to ignore. He urged her to share her story with him, and after twenty minutes, Felix was so angry he was afraid he might reveal his true self to the young woman.

He felt the need to protect her, to help her right the wrongs in her life. Felix knew that letting her talk about it would help, but what she needed was a change of scenery. Staying here with her so-called friends was not going to help her, so he did the only thing he could. He gave her his information and asked her to apply for an internship with him at MacDonald Estate.

Not only would it give her something to focus on and help her out of the hole she had dug for herself, but it also benefited Felix to have someone too distracted with themselves to focus on the excavation. Gretchen would like a change of pace, and Maura's grave would possibly be safer with students who were looking for an escape from the ordinary more than making any significant discovery. Felix made a mental note to e-mail his assistant to put Gretchen's application at the front of the pile.

CHAPTER 1

Gretchen Jones compared the map in her hands to the landscape in front of her. The main house seemed overwhelming and pretentious in its stone design. It stood like a fortress, in the center of everything, the grounds surrounding it manicured to perfection and the wood at the back side of the property obscured the drop of a very steep cliff edge. The cliff was the only area not surrounded by a massive stone wall.

The MacDonald Estate, Felix had explained to her when she first arrived, was built to keep the world out (or people in, if the rumors were to be believed). The grid she was considering was located about half way between the main house and the edge of the wood. She was in the middle of surveying the section to excavate, when she heard Janet's flirtatious giggle from behind her. The high-pitched bubbles of sound carried far in the chill of early evening. It was almost time to pack up for the day. Shaking her head, she marked a promising grid on her map.

Janet had always been easily distracted by the opposite sex. Hearing Janet's giggling again, Gretchen looked up and spotted Janet chatting it up with a man who most definitely wasn't one of the people working on the site. Frustrated, she set down her map and made her way over to the duo. Ever since Felix's disappearance, the original group of interns had lost what little work ethic they had. Not that she could blame them.

Working under Declan Murray was punishing, to say the least. Sure, he had made the first major discovery since the first network of passages had been found inside the main house, but everyone was over his Indiana Jones attitude. Even after finding nothing of importance in the room he discovered, he pushed everyone like a slave driver. With any luck, they would discover another room soon, and this time not an empty one.

That should get Declan off their backs for a bit. Not that he was overly micromanaging during the day, in fact, he was quite absentee, but when he did grace them with his unwelcome presence, the mood on the site turned glacial at best. Just thinking about Declan replacing Felix in any way made her heart hurt.

It was only now that Felix was gone that she had been able to admit how close they had gotten over the last two years. Dr. Felix Aiken had been tall and handsome, but it was his enthusiasm for the MacDonald Estate that had swept her away. He had been a true intellectual, not the playboy type she'd hung around in her early college days. Another fit of giggling interrupted her thoughts, and she continued on her path. This was still an active excavation, not a tourist attraction. If Janet's friend was here for any reason other than business, she would have to escort him out.

As she approached, Gretchen studied the man Janet was with. While Janet was flaunting her smile and ample bosom, the man didn't even seem to notice. His handsome yet slightly gaunt face was serious as he talked, and Gretchen wasn't quite close enough to make out exactly what the conversation was about. If Janet's puzzled expression was anything to go by, the man wasn't buying what she was so obviously offering.

"Can I help you sir?" Gretchen asked, intruding on their mostly one-sided conversation.

The man looked relieved that there was someone new to the conversation as he introduced himself, "Dr. Shane Pearse. I am a colleague of Dr. Felix Aiken."

He extended his hand for her to shake, and Gretchen took it. His hand felt a little cold in hers, even given the chill in the air, but he didn't look like he was in full health at the moment.

"Gretchen Jones. What brings you to MacDonald Estate?" She cut to the chase.

A few people had visited claiming to know Felix in order to see if there was anything of value around the site. She didn't have time for games, but after a few more questions, Dr. Pearce seemed legitimately interested in what was going on. Janet tried to get Dr. Pearse's attention, but again Gretchen steered the conversation back to the dig and what they had found. Janet seemed to get bored with the conversation quickly now that it seemed Dr. Pearse wasn't interested in anything more than the progress on the dig.

"Like I was saying, Dr. Aiken may not have been super-motivated as far as progress on the dig, but he taught us a lot otherwise. I just don't understand why he would just up and leave. I don't believe he would do that willingly, and I definitely don't understand him putting Declan in charge. Everyone knew they didn't get along in the least. Not that Declan is a very personable person. He wasn't even here for the experience. He gave me more of a treasure hunter vibe than a serious archaeologist," Gretchen blurted before she could catch herself. She bit her lip and blushed.

Gretchen wasn't the gossiping type, at least not anymore. She really needed to get her emotions in check. Dr. Pearse wasn't the first person to come asking about Felix, but for some reason she felt comfortable giving him more information than what was necessary. Almost like the first time she had met Felix, she found herself spilling her guts without reservation.

"So, when was the last time you saw Dr. Aiken?" Dr. Pearse asked, and she sighed.

"He usually kept to himself after the work day was over. The last time I saw him, we had convinced him to join us out at Uisge Beatha, it's a local pub named after the Scottish national drink. The place is a dive, but the drinks are cheap. Anyway, that was the night before the room was discovered. Everyone was there, well except Declan, but no one minded since he was usually a drag. Dr. Aiken left early and in a hurry like he had forgotten an appointment or something. I only remember because he practically knocked me over on his way to the door," Gretchen said, and Dr. Pearse nodded.

"Did Declan ever show up that night?" he asked, and she shook her head.

"No, but like I said that wasn't unusual for Declan. He always thought he was better than all of us and rarely hung out with anyone. He was too focused on finding buried treasure and hated Dr. Aiken for stalling him in finding his fortune. Declan seriously thought he was on the verge of discovering the fountain of youth. Surprisingly, he took it rather well when it turned out to be an empty room," Gretchen said.

Dr. Pearse nodded and asked a few more questions about the progress on the dig before excusing himself to find Declan. She was almost glad, though she had been at ease around Dr. Pearse, she hadn't been okay with how easily she had lost her professionalism. With a shake of her head, Gretchen went back to the workstation where she left her map and noticed an envelope that hadn't been there before.

"What is this?" she asked a passing intern.

He shrugged and kept going, so she picked up the envelope and opened it. It was the lab results from the soil samples. A small jolt of excitement went through her, they would finally know the secret to the red dirt. Declan had been against her sending them, but she had anyway. The soil composition was valuable archaeological data, especially given the strange red hue the whole room seemed to have.

It was completely different from any other area surrounding the room. Her excitement died as she read the results. A chill crept up her spine that had nothing to do with the weather. Now they knew why the soil was red, it was saturated with blood. Gretchen shoved the results back into the envelope and stuck it into her back pocket. These results would be going straight to the authorities as soon as she was done here.

The sun was getting low, and everyone was starting to wrap things up for the day. MacDonald Estate might be impressive and well-manicured during the day, but at night, it could easily be used in a horror film. The massive stone walls cast ominous shadows in the moonlight. Not to mention the evidence of foul play burning a hole through her pocket.

She was busy securing her things for the night when she saw Declan approaching. He wore his usual scowl as he headed directly for her. He seemed even more menacing since Dr. Aiken's disappearance than he had before. It was evident in the way people jumped to get out of his way and refused to look in his eyes as he passed.

"I thought I told you to direct all further excavation to the north of the site," he snarled at her, coming to a stop well within her personal bubble.

As much as she wanted to take a step back, she didn't dare move. There was no way she would allow Declan to see just how much he bothered her.

"That doesn't make any sense and we both know it. It's clear that there should be more tunnel headed toward the house not away from it," she said. It might not be entirely true, there could be more tunnels leading away from the estate house but surely finding a connection to the house would benefit the funding of the site for future excavations. Declan may be a hot head, but he wasn't an idiot.

He ran a hand through his hair as he often did when agitated.

"Anyway, I wanted to discuss a few issues with site management."

"We've made a lot of progress in the older sections," she supplied, but his scowl only deepened.

"Not about that," he spat running his hand through his hair again.

Gretchen glanced around, noticing that everyone had stopped what they were doing to watch their exchange.

"Maybe we should go someplace away from the others."

She preferred to have this discussion without an audience. Their rivalry was legendary and the last thing she needed was for a spat with Declan to end up in a report somewhere and jeopardize her position at the site. He glared down at her for a second before stalking off in the direction of the wood. She had no choice, but to follow. It wasn't until they got far enough from the others not to be heard that she stopped.

"This is far enough," she said.

It was one thing to be out of earshot of the others, but she didn't want to be out of their sightline. She stopped where she was, but Declan grabbed her roughly by the arm. His grip was so tight that it stung even through the padding of her thick sweater. He began to drag her closer to the woods edge, and Gretchen panicked.

"Declan, stop! What the hell is wrong with you? Let me go!" Gretchen yelled, but his grip only tightened as he dragged her into the trees.

She pulled with all her might, but Declan was stronger than she had thought. Turning back, she could see that there was no one looking in their direction. Still she waved her free arm, hoping someone, anyone would see and come to her aid. When she realized they were too close to the wood, far enough away that her waving and screams were for naught, she renewed her full efforts to get away.

Mentally, Gretchen cursed herself for being so stupid. She should have learned her lesson from Justin. All men had ulterior motives and Declan Murphy was no exception. Declan had never cared about other people's feelings and it seemed he'd decided he wanted something from her and he was going to take it. All the time she had spent in self-defense classes had failed her in her struggle against him. If anything, she only managed to drain her own energy, but she refused to give up. She refused to be a victim, not this time. She continued to fight as he dragged her further into the dense foliage. At this rate, it seemed he might lead them both off the cliff.

"Let go!" she cried again, giving yet another tug, but he pulled her against him so that they were face to face.

"Not until I've had my fill," he growled, his lips curling up revealing a set of sharp fangs.

Her body tensed in fear; her mouth open, prepared to scream, but he was too quick. Before her mind could comprehend her situation, she felt a sharp pain in her neck and then he was gone. She collapsed, her breathing ragged, she tried not to panic at the massive amount of blood pooling around her.

Gretchen lay stunned as she watched the most beautiful man she had ever seen beat the living daylights out of Declan. Even the cold seeping into her bones from the forest floor couldn't diminish the warmth in her heart as she watched her blond guardian angel.

She was dying. Her blood poured from her body, leaving her weak and hopeless. The only thing keeping her lucid was the searing fireball of pain that was her throat. A part of her was glad he was getting punished for what he had done to her, but the other half was petrified. She only managed a moan of thanks before the world began to slip away.

❅❅❅

LANGSMITH, CALIFORNIA
SIX MONTHS LATER

Maura was furious. Declan was way too reckless, and without her power, she could do nothing to stop it. This sense of helplessness wasn't something she ever wanted to feel. Sure, she had witnessed the emotion in the men and women she had drained over the years, but to actually feel it herself? Maura had every intention of getting rid of it. Even without her dark magic, she wasn't completely powerless. She was an ancient Vampire with many tricks left up her sleeve.

She caught a glance of herself in the mirror left

hanging on the peeling walls of her new hideout. She stopped in disgust. Without her dark magic, the effect of the blood she so carefully harvested wasn't holding up as long as she needed. Deep creases at the corners of her mouth and eyes marred her once flawless visage. Even the jet black of her hair was fading to a pale gray. Soon her strength would begin to diminish, as well. As if her dreary surrounding weren't enough to put her in a bad mood.

The hasty retreat from the MacDonald Estate had landed them briefly in an American motel. She'd stayed in a few rat-infested shit holes in her day, but never had she paid to stay in one. That wasn't an experience she would ever repeat.

This place was only a minor step up, fully furnished in a tasteless hunting theme. The most suitable place Declan could come up with on such short notice, and limited funds. Maura needed to build not only her army, but her fortune. In the meantime, she was forced to endure this squalor. No doubt some hunter's cabin.

Staring into the glass eyes of the dead moose head hung above the fireplace, she could see the appeal of having one's trophy kills mounted on the walls. An idea she might take into consideration when she completed her revenge. The only real bonus of the cabin was its location, hidden by forest in the mountains near the last known location of her targets.

Declan was most certainly going to pay for his incompetence. It was his fault Molly was gone, and so was the necklace, the key to all of her power. Molly had seemed like the perfect tool for her revenge. Maura had used a lot of her magic to get Molly's head back on her body and bring her back to life. Shane had always been weak, and using his not so dead lover against him would have brought him down in no time.

Molly had been delightfully gullible, falling for everything Maura said about Shane abandoning her. She'd had no idea of Maura's true intentions until Declan let his dick do his thinking. She'd had all three members of her old army exactly where she had wanted them, but Declan's obsession with that Gretchen girl got the better of him. He'd attacked her without Maura's permission, and things had gone downhill from there. With a huff, Maura made her way down the hall to the room where Declan waited.

She shoved the door open and glared down at him. Declan shivered as a cold breeze swept through the room and over his healing form. It was taking a lot longer for him to heal than Maura anticipated. If she gave him some of her blood, Declan would be as good as new in no time. Not that she would, his pain was his punishment for ruining her plans. Declan sat up and smirked. Even on the edge of death, he reeked of arrogance.

"I'd say it is lovely to see you, but I'm not one for white lies. You're a few feedings short I'd say."

Maura's hands curled into fists so tight she was sure blood was being drawn. Declan flinched visibly as if her anger was a physical object and she had just slapped him with it. That thought calmed her just a little. Maura had only felt more insulted one other time in her long life. Claude had learned his lesson, and now it was time Declan learned his. He had outworn his welcome. As soon as he was completely healed, she would use him to help rebuild her army. Then she would end his miserable existence as a lesson to the others about loyalty.

"Go feed," Maura ordered, ignoring his comment, "I don't need you to die before you've been of any use."

"Yes, my Queen." Declan replied, but his sarcastic

tone wasn't lost on Maura.

She narrowed her eyes at him before leaving him in the room alone. Declan had once been a convenient ally, but he hadn't lasted long before his personal entanglements ruined her carefully laid plans. That annoying Gretchen woman; Declan had talked incessantly about her ever since his turning. If she hadn't been well known amongst the students, Maura would have demanded her as a sacrifice that first day.

Declan had truly disappointed her with his rash actions, and she had exercised great restraint in his punishment. She was sure he would find more ways to disappoint her. However, given that under his watch not only had her powers gone missing, but the key to her plan for revenge had taken off as well, she had no idea how much worse he could get. Even the traitors who had tried to kill her had been more competent than Declan Murray.

Maura would have to be more careful with the rest of her new army. She reached the door to her room only to pause. The cabin was too quiet. Her latest recruits should have roused themselves by now. She turned and headed back down the hall, stopping at the second door. It flew open just as her hand touched the knob, and she was faced with the scrawny, weasel-faced Rodney.

"Come to check on us?"

His voice was nasally and grating, but she had witnessed firsthand his way with words. Rodney had interrupted Maura in her feeding on his brother, Axel. It was his mouth that had saved his pitiful life. He convinced Maura that he could be of more use than his strong, but lack wit brother alone.

"Just ensuring my newest members survived the night."

"All's well and dandy with us, but I think you would

prefer a little better accommodations?”

Maura raised a brow in question and the man smiled.

“I’ll get right on it,” he said and closed the door in her face.

At the moment she didn’t have the capacity to be offended, all her anger was still focused on Declan and her current situation. Something Rodney had apparently picked up on. He was a sly one. Someone she would have to keep her eyes on. Maybe even more so than Declan.

CHAPTER 2

"**I** can't believe we just watched a marathon of teen Vampire movies. Whose idea was this anyway?" Gretchen groaned, sitting up in the way too comfy recliner.

She'd woken up right before the credits rolled on the last film. She glanced over to see Cat and Molly exchange glances before bursting into laughter. In the last four months, Gretchen had come to enjoy the company of the unlikely best friends.

"Sweetheart, the only thing you were watching was something steamy involving Claude," Cat said, and Gretchen blushed.

Okay, so she'd been dreaming about a real Vampire. A sexy one and a very off limits one, but how did they know that? As far as she knew no one here could read minds.

"I don't know what you are talking about," she said, and they giggled before Cat grabbed Molly.

"Oh, Claude!" Molly cried and proceeded to swoon as Cat pretended to kiss her.

Embarrassed that she had obviously been talking in her sleep, Gretchen grabbed a handful of her discarded popcorn and threw it at them.

"Stop, alright. So what? It was better than sparkly Vampires."

"Hey, this is my bachelorette party. We get to do what I want." Cat adjusted the fake princess crown on her head.

Molly rolled her eyes.

"Anything except leaving the compound and hire a male stripper. Doesn't anyone else see how cult-like this all is? Three women stuck in a high-security compound with three men." Molly complained.

"Don't go there, Molly. It's only heavily guarded because Maura is still out there. You wouldn't feel so caged up if you would just forgive Shane already." Cat sighed.

"Don't start this again. He betrayed me." Molly sat up in her chair.

Not one to back down on anything, Cat sat up as well. "Oh, I'm starting it all right. You and Shane are meant to be 'together forever' if I recall correctly."

Things were going downhill fast. The issues needed to be talked out, there was no doubt about that, but Gretchen knew now was not the time. This was supposed to be fun girl time before Cat and Xander's wedding tomorrow.

"It was more like till death do we part. I died; it's over."

"Did you think you weren't going to die if he turned you? Hello! Vampires are undead. What the hell happened that made you so—so—jaded?"

"Actually, we were half dead when they turned us," Gretchen muttered. Cat shot her a menacing glare.

"What happened? You know damn well what happened," Molly spoke over her.

The two best friends stared each other down. The tension in the room was palpable, and Gretchen knew she needed to interject before things truly went sour.

"Listen up, you two. We agreed no serious talk tonight. We are supposed to be having fun," she interrupted their bickering.

They both glared at her for a moment before sighing and taking in the mess that they had created in Shane's theater room. Decorating the space with pink and white streamers and crepe paper had been fun, but now, after the festive feeling had left, all it looked like was unwelcome work.

"It's late, you should all get some rest," a disembodied voice said causing them all to jump.

The girls searched the room only for Shane to emerge from a shadowed corner by the door. Gretchen relaxed a little, but not completely. Shane was a nice guy, but he could really give a girl the creeps sometimes. He looked almost nothing like the man Gretchen had met at the estate. Dr. Pearse had been somewhat gaunt in appearance, but he'd still had color in his cheeks and life in his eyes. The man standing in front of her now was well—his eyes were sunken and with barely any spark of life in them. His skin was pale and hung from his bony frame as if he were a malnourished child. If he'd been wearing a hooded cloak, he could pass as death itself.

"We'll go after we clean up," Cat said.

Gretchen nodded in agreement, but Molly just scoffed and stormed out of the room.

Shane's eyes tracked her every movement, but as soon as she was gone the brief glimpse of light in his eyes vanished.

"No, I will clean up. Consider it my wedding present," he said, and Cat smiled at him before getting up and giving him a big hug.

"Thanks Shane," she said before leaving as well.

Gretchen stood and started tearing down the crepe. The others might be okay with leaving the mess, but she wasn't. Molly was a bit of a prima donna, Cat was a permanent resident, but Gretchen was just a guest. Well, more like refugee, at least until she learned to manage Vampire life on her own.

"You don't have to," Shane began, but Gretchen shot him a look.

"I don't know all the details about what's going on with you and Molly, but you really need to start taking better care of yourself. How is she supposed to remember the man she fell in love with when you walk around looking like death?"

He seemed struck by her words, but said nothing as he began to clean as well. The next twenty minutes was spent working in a companionable silence.

"I'll make you a deal." Shane bagged up the last of the trash.

"What?"

"I'll take your advice into consideration if you take Claude into consideration."

"That is not a fair deal."

"I never said it was," he said and left her in the room alone.

Gretchen sighed and picked up the remaining trash bag to take out. Shane was one odd character. With the clean-up done, she headed for her room. It really was late, and she didn't want to be too exhausted to help Cat out with the final details for the ceremony tomorrow.

She was just about to reach the stairs when she saw Claude coming from the opposite direction. His head bent as he ran a towel over his sandy blond hair. His chest was bare, giving her the perfect view of his slim muscled figure, glistening with moisture.

Gretchen took back her comment about sparkly

Vampires. This was one she wouldn't mind getting her hands on. She was too busy ogling him to realize she had continued walking past the stairs until she almost ran into him. She quickly backpedaled, only to lose her footing and begin to fall. He reached out catching her in his arms before she hit the floor, but instead of just helping her up he maneuvered her against the wall. Trapping her against it with his body.

"You should be more careful," he said giving her a killer smile.

Being this close, she could smell the mixture of chlorine and sweat on his skin. She was completely unprepared to deal with this onslaught of sexy. To think she had thought him an angel on their first meeting. Granted, she'd been dealing with a severe lack of blood at the time.

"I was just going to bed," she stammered and silently cursed herself for showing even that much weakness in his presence.

In the few months she'd been holed up in the mansion with him, she'd learned her angel was, in fact, a chauvinistic womanizer. Not exactly the type of man one should be involved with while dealing with a personal trauma. She took a deep breath and forced herself to look him in the eyes. Their hazel depths gleamed with wicked intent.

"Ah, I'd be happy to join you."

Focus, Gretch. Don't let him in. You don't need this. Mind over matter, young lady.

"Oh, I'm sure you would."

Wait, what? That's flirting, no flirting. Just leave before you go too far.

"It's no secret that I want you, Gretchen." He fondled a curly lock of her hair.

There was no doubting the chemistry between them,

but she wasn't ready to give in.

"I'm not interested in being one of your many conquests."

> *Yes! Just like that. Keep up the good work, Gretch.*

"What if I told you I wanted more than just one night? That you could never be just a simple conquest."

The sincerity in his voice was almost her undoing. He leaned in closer his lips hovering over hers, waiting for her to make the next move. The ball was in her court now. If she just leaned in, gave in, and took what he offered, would she be able to get him out of her system? Her body was screaming for her to go for it, but in the end, it was her mind that made the final decision.

> *No, no one night stands either. There is no telling how long you will be stuck here.*

"What makes you think if something did happen between us that I would want more than just one night? You are such an arrogant ass. Don't ever dare to think you know what I want."

She closed the gap between them. Her lips pressed softly against his for a brief moment before she pushed him away and ran up to her room. As relieved as she felt with the encounter being over, part of her was having a pity party. She only hoped she wouldn't regret rejecting his proposal in the morning.

❈❈❈

Claude stood stunned as he watched Gretchen practically sprint away from him. To be honest his words to her had surprised even him. He'd known he'd lusted for her, but it wasn't until he'd held her in his arms that an uncomfortable warmth had spread in his chest. He actually cared for the sassy, little mouse.

She had a way of keeping him on his toes that no other woman had managed in his long life, not even Maura.

Not wanting to be found half naked with a hard on in the middle of the night, he headed for his own room. Even after that sweet, stinging rejection, he would need a cold shower to alleviate his discomfort. He paused as he passed Gretchen's room. He could hear her moving around inside. She was getting into bed judging by the shifting sound of linen and the slight creak of mattress springs. Despite his better judgment, he stood there listening, imagining her movements.

He stopped breathing when he realized her movements had a rhythmic quality to them. He moved closer to her door, picking up on her soft moans he found himself cupping his own erection. Matching the slide of his hand with her intimate cadence. Her breathing increased as did her movement and the barest hint of her aroused scent tickled his nostrils. He knew she was close as her breathing became labored and erratic.

"Claude!" He could have sworn she whispered in the height of her own completion.

Losing what little control he had over his own actions, he tightened and released his grip as he stroked himself, mimicking the spasmodic contractions of the female orgasm. He placed one hand on the door to steady himself as he finished, making a mess in his swim trunks. Claude cursed under his breath. The release had only been a temporary solution. He hadn't experienced such uncontrollable lust since his teen years.

I must be completely out of my mind.

He quickly walked the two doors down to his own room and slammed the door shut behind him. His predicament was calamitous. This would not do at all.

He had to find some solution. He stripped off his swim trunks and deposited them in the trash. There was no way he could wear those again. Claude needed a plan, but first he really needed that cold shower.

❈❈❈

After the appalling end to her bachelorette party, Cat had tried her best to take Shane's advice and get some rest. Despite her best efforts, nothing had worked. It was the night before her wedding, of course Cat couldn't sleep. She spent the past three hours nervously pacing her room until she was sure everyone else had gone to bed.

Cat hadn't been able to keep herself from thinking about the million different ways for the day to end in disaster. Her dress might become inexplicably ruined, Molly and Shane would most definitely get into an argument, and Xander would be displeased about the decorations if they weren't perfect.

There was so much that could go wrong. Worse than anything else, Maura could attack, and everyone would be so caught off guard that it would end in mass bloodshed and death. Cat didn't want to think about any of it anymore. Maybe a change of scenery would work. She left her room and made her way to the courtyard where everything was all set for the wedding.

As much as the boys talked about hating the MacDonald Estate, they had moved into what was possibly the closest thing to a replica of it as they could find.

Cat hadn't been able to resist looking up the place after the men had all but abandoned her on their reckless quest for the woman who had previously tortured the living daylights out of them. The mansion, although much smaller than the estate, had a similar stone fortress feel from the outside. It even had towers at each corner of the house.

It was the inside of the mansion that they had truly made their home. Each of them had their own corner decorated to suit their personality and era, even if they didn't realize it. Xander and Claude's spaces were filled with impressive antiques and very sparse modern conveniences, while Shane's area looked like the sixties and seventies had a baby.

Everything was dated except his movie room, and other than the kitchen, it was the most modern space in the house. The garden out back and even the center courtyard had an old-world charm to it. You could almost forget you were in the mountains of California.

The slight chill in the air made Cat shiver and wish she had put on her robe instead of traipsing around in the vintage silk nightgown Molly had insisted she wear as the bride-to-be. Taking everything in, Cat felt herself relax a little. The courtyard was breathtaking even in the light of the full moon. The flowers were all perfectly placed and except for a few last-minute details everything was exactly as it should be. It gave her hope that maybe things would be okay after all.

"Everything will be just fine," a familiar voice said from behind Cat.

Startled, Cat turned quickly, nearly losing her footing. She managed to catch herself in time, but the sight of the shadowy figure had her stumbling once again. The first time The Shadow had visited her, she had thought she was going crazy. As if being a Vampire wasn't enough, now she saw ghosts.

Although the ghost had no real form or features, Cat was pretty sure the ghostly shadow was Xander's first love, Rachel. Not that The Shadow ever gave any hint to its true identity. It just randomly showed up one night and scared the crap out of Cat with a creepy photo montage and a cryptic message about Maura's plans for revenge.

"Jesus! What do you want?"

"Don't worry. I am not here to hurt you."

"No, you just like to scare the living daylights out of me. Can a girl get a little warning sometime?"

The dark figure laughed and crossed the space, getting closer to her until she was almost certain she could feel The Shadow's breath.

"I don't know why. I have done nothing but help you."

"Help me?"

Cat put her hand on her hip. Her eyebrow raised in question and a bit of challenge.

"Yes, help you. If I hadn't given you the necklace and explained its purpose, you would have no hope of getting rid of Maura."

"It's because you gave me this thing that I constantly live with the threat of her attack! What made you think that giving me the key to Maura's power was a good idea?"

"Trust me, you are safer with it than without it. This is not what I came to discuss. You and Alexander have found each other, and your love has weakened the dark magic in the necklace, but there is still a long way to go."

"What do you mean?"

"Claude and Shane must also find love for you to be free, and for Maura to be destroyed once and for all."

"Well, that should be easy." Cat rolled her eyes.

"Just like you have, they must find their own fairytale endings."

"Seriously? Are you supposed to be a fairy godmother?

If so, you are doing a horrible job. I mean, really? Where were you when Felix got ripped to shreds by Maura? What about when Shane went off the deep end because the last he saw of Molly was her head separated from her body? Not to mention when Gretchen got her throat ripped out by Declan! I'm sorry, but you are more than just a day late and a dollar short. Even if I could help, how am I supposed to work through that shit storm?"

If a shadow had features, Cat was sure there was a death glare boring into her at that moment. She could almost feel it heating her body despite the cool night air. The Shadow was something else. It only came to demand things of Cat that were completely insane.

It seemed to know just about everything except the fact that Cat had already tried her hand playing matchmaker for Shane and Claude. After all, Molly and Shane were meant to be "together forever", but it would take a lot more than just Cat to get those two past their issues.

Then there was the issue of Claude. He may be charming, but love was definitely not in his vocabulary. Gretchen would be the perfect match, with her no-nonsense attitude, but wanted nothing to do with him. Cat just wasn't the type to be overly pushy about romantic entanglements.

"Just figure something out!"

"It's not for me to figure out! I don't know who or what you are, but you definitely don't know anything about love!"

Almost as soon as the words were out of her mouth, Cat felt the urge to take them back. If The Shadow really was Xander's ex, Cat had seriously put her foot in her mouth. There was bound to be some bad karma coming her way. She reached out to The Shadow, but it disappeared, leaving Cat alone once again to her thoughts. Maybe it was time to tell the others about The Shadow's visits. Okay, maybe just Xander. Tonight, however, wasn't the time.

CHAPTER 3

Claude held his breath to combat the giant yawn building in his throat. Xander had spared no expense filling the courtyard with fragrant flowers and elegant decorations. Cat was stunning in her long, white princess gown, and Xander looked her perfect match in a white tuxedo with gold trim. It was exactly like the fairy tale Beauty and the Beast. As beautiful as everything was, it was completely unnecessary.

Xander had been claiming Cat all over the house for weeks now. You would think Xander would have given up on the more antiquated traditions by now. Besides, if it were truly a traditional ceremony, it should have been him giving away the bride. He was her sire and therefore she was his to give away. Cat had laughed in his face when he'd suggested it.

The only interesting part of the whole wedding was watching Gretchen pretending she wasn't into this sappy love fest. He couldn't seem to keep his eyes off of her, even as Xander and Cat said their vows. Claude sat transfixed as a single tear trailed across Gretchen's flushed cheek, quickly followed by another.

He hated weeping women. It was normally a blatant attempt to gain attention, but she was an exception. The way she tried to hide the fact that she was so emotionally invested in the situation by quickly swiping away at her cheeks, endeared him to her even more. Leaning across the aisle, he pulled out his handkerchief and offered it to her. Not even looking at him, she accepted it, delicately dabbing at the tiny drops of moisture streaming down her face.

Claude swallowed hard when she dabbed closer to her mouth. His eyes drawn to one of her best features, her lips. Pale pink and trembling with each shaky breath she took; he was at a loss. His manhood strained against the fabric of his pants as he imagined how they might feel against his skin. He could have stared at them for hours, but the sound of clapping reached his sex-addled brain.

He forced his attention back to the ceremony and the happy couple, who were now sharing their first kiss as man and wife. Finally, they were getting to the good part. It would soon be time for dancing, and Claude was anxious to have a chance to have Gretchen in his arms.

"It's time for the couple's first dance," Claude announced before starting the stereo that would be playing the music for the evening.

Xander had wanted a real orchestra, but letting strangers into the compound wasn't a risk anyone was willing to take. Maura and Declan were still out there, and there was no telling when they would strike. Despite the looming threat, the ceremony had been beautiful and thankfully uneventful.

The grandeur of Cat and Xander's wedding was a bit absurd for the small group in attendance, in Claude's opinion, but Xander had insisted. Xander extended his hand to Cat, who took it blushing slightly as he swung her into his arms. Claude fought the gag rising in his throat. He much preferred it when Cat was taking Xander down a notch or two, not acting the smitten bride. The love between the newlywed couple was absolutely stifling as it filled the night air.

After the couple had their first dance, Claude made a beeline for Gretchen. He had been waiting all night to get her into his arms, and nothing was going to stop him. Except maybe Shane, because before Claude could get across the room, he was leading her out to the floor. Claude cursed under his breath, but he would be patient. He had waited all night; one song longer would be nothing.

***

"Thank you," Gretchen said as she stepped into Shane's arms.

She carefully placed her hand in his, and he started to move. Slowly, following the music, they floated around the dance floor. Gretchen had been relieved when Shane had asked her to dance. She'd been avoiding Claude and his lecherous gaze all night. She knew he wouldn't hesitate to coerce her into his arms. Shane was a good dancer, but Gretchen figured he'd had plenty of time to practice.

"No, Gretchen, thank you. It's an honor to dance with such a stunning woman, especially one that isn't openly plotting my demise," Shane said making Gretchen laugh out loud.

Gretchen chose to ignore the glare Claude was shooting in Shane's direction. Although his jealous act was cute in a way. It was bad enough with the daggers of Molly's eyes in Shane's back. Gretchen tried to be a good partner, but it seemed Shane couldn't help that his attention was drawn to Molly.

"Just give her time. A lot has happened, and she's just trying to sort things out. To be honest if I were in her place I'd be just as pissed off," Gretchen said.

Shane nodded curtly. Obviously, he hadn't liked her opinion on the matter. Instead, he focused on the dance. He swung Gretchen out to spin her around and finished it with a dip. She laughed again, but as quickly as her laughter had come, it died almost immediate. Claude was crossing the room towards them, and the determination in his face was enough to kill her good mood. She had honestly hoped to avoid all contact with Claude until their archery lesson tomorrow, but apparently, he had other plans.

Shane graciously bowed out leaving her to fend for herself. A slight smile tugged at his lips as he glided away. She had no time to react as she was pulled tightly against Claude's muscled form and swept into motion.

❈❈❈

Molly smiled as her best friend twirled around the dance floor with her new husband. Despite their argument last night, she wasn't angry. The two had never been able to stay mad at each other for long. Even when Maura had sworn that Shane and Cat had betrayed her, Molly hadn't been able to hold a grudge.

Okay, so maybe she'd gone too far with that creepy dream spell, but Molly had been sure of her friend's betrayal up until that point. The pleading in Cat's voice as she'd called after Molly in the darkness hadn't been a guilty one, but a worried one. It had been the first sign that things might not be what Maura and Declan had made them seem.

Feeling awkward standing alone at the edge of the dance floor, she took a seat at an empty table. Shane had decided to ask Gretchen to dance, and Molly hated to admit that she felt even the slightest pang of jealousy because of it. Instead, she decided it was proof of his lack of devotion to her.

He stalked her and hovered around her, but other than that had made no move to show that he had even an ounce of the love they had once shared left. Shane had changed, just as she had, and it hurt seeing him so consumed with himself. He was a shell of the man he once was, and Molly was sure it had more to do with his own demons than any grief or remorse he felt at losing her.

Molly frowned as Shane twirled Gretchen and finished with an extravagant dip. Anger welled up inside of her. They had never danced like that. In fact, Shane had made it a point to avoid any situation that would require him to dance. Claude stormed across the room, breaking up the pair. He had it bad, and everyone knew it.

Gretchen was so out of depth with his aggressive courtship, but anyone who had known Claude longer than a few months knew that his tactics with Gretchen were not his norm. If she were any other women, he would be more aloof and charming and not the raging dickhead he'd proven himself to be in front of her. It was quite entertaining to watch even if Molly felt a little sorry for her.

❈❈❈

Claude wasn't used to the jealous feeling that had radiated through him as he watched Gretchen dancing and laughing with Shane. He'd wanted to punch Shane in the face as the man had let his hand drift slightly lower on the curve of her hip. Claude knew Shane was only taunting him, but it had only increased his possessiveness. He knew he was officially a goner when he instantly felt better once Gretchen was firmly in his arms, even if she insisted on fighting him.

He knew her body was reacting to his being near, just as his was reacting to hers. From the moment he had seen her, something had drawn him to her. He still wasn't sure exactly what it was, not that he had ever been picky about women. She wasn't overly pretty, definitely not a model, but more the girl next door type.

Tonight, she had tamed her curly mass of hair by pulling it up into some kind of twisted up-do. It was a shame as he had fully intended on getting his hands in those brown spirals as he kissed those perfectly shaped lips of hers. From what he could tell she hadn't used any makeup, and yet her eyes held his attention almost as much as her lips.

He pulled Gretchen closer, slowing the movement of his hips, until he was sure she felt just how much he wanted her. Gretchen squirmed against him under the guise of being free of him, but the shallow, choppy nature of her breathing and the rosy flush of her cheeks told him otherwise. Yes, this was definitely worth the holes she was boring into his chest with those big gray eyes of hers.

Despite his raging hormones, he kept his hands in check; one at the small of her back, a respectful distance from her heart shaped bottom, and the other firmly grasping her small delicate hand. The last time he had held her hand it had been a lot rougher, calloused from digging and whatever other hard labor she had done before the attack.

"If you keep squirming like that, I will be forced to abscond with you to my room," Claude breathed into her ear.

His fangs ached with the need to bite her as he was so close to her neck. Even hidden under the fabric of her dress. Claude had been appalled when he'd seen that her dress was also a turtleneck. Her style of choice because of the scar left by that bastard Declan. That reminder had Claude pulling back, but the heated look in Gretchen's eyes made him abandon all thoughts of chivalry.

***

Gretchen stilled at Claude's threat. In all her life Gretchen had never felt so needy. Her body was tempted to keep wiggling just so that he would, but her brain was fully in control. Claude was exactly the kind of guy she didn't need to be around. Especially with everything else she was dealing with right now. He was a predator and she, unfortunately, was his prey of choice at the moment. She just had to keep reminding herself of that fact.

"Ordinarily, people live and learn, you, on the other hand, seem content with just living," Gretchen said with a sweet smile that surely wasn't reflective of her mood.

She pushed her body away from his and stormed out of the room. She hadn't wanted to make a scene on Cat's big day, but Claude had forced her hand. The whole ceremony had been increasingly awkward as he had stared at her, making his intentions clear from across the room. Claude wanted her, and he would stop at nothing until he had her. Gretchen's body was restless with desire; all she needed was a few nights of lusty adventure, but that was not what Claude had to offer. He had made that clear from the beginning. He wanted complete surrender, her complete surrender.

To make matters worse, Gretchen wasn't sure that what he had to offer wasn't what she wanted. It would be so easy to fall in love with a sexy Vampire like Claude, but if Gretchen had learned anything in life, it was that things were never as easy as they seemed. Gretchen was still trying to realize her true self. A journey she had been on even before the dramatic event that had changed her life forever.

If she had thought finding herself was hard before, finding herself while dealing with Vampirism was on a whole new level of difficult; a level she didn't want to further complicate with emotional entanglement. Then, there was Claude's reputation. What made her so different from the countless other women he had seduced and used? Why was it only now and only with her that he wanted more?

Gretchen stumbled a little as she missed a step. With a curse, she stopped to pull off her heels before continuing up the stairs to her room. She was glad that no one had followed her as she closed her bedroom door. She didn't feel like dealing with getting the third degree from Cat or Molly, or worse Claude.

She stripped down to her underwear and crawled into bed. Dealing with Claude, as always, had been exhausting. Her body and mind were constantly at war whenever she was around him. It was maddening. She reached for the book on her nightstand, but found she couldn't focus long enough to read it. Her mind kept drifting to the moment she wished she could forget. She reached up and touched the scar on her neck where Declan had ripped her throat out. Despite the healing power of Vampirism, the scar remained stubbornly as a reminder of her ultimate failure in judgment.

Every time she had a moment to herself her mind always drifted back to that day. If it weren't for that scar and her current situation, she would think it was all some horrible dream. Gretchen had no clue to the depth of Maura's evil, but to her, no one could be worse than Declan Murray. He'd been a thorn in her side since the day she met him. If only she had known before it was too late that he not only was an arrogant prick, but a freaking murderous Vampire slave. If she ever ran across Declan Murray again, she would kill him herself.

❈❈❈

Shane watched for a moment as the newlywed couples swayed to the music. While Claude and Gretchen rushed off after fighting, Xander and Cat floated effortlessly across the floor, smiling and laughing together. The grand ceremony served a dual purpose. First and most importantly, to give Cat the fairytale wedding she had never wanted, but fully deserved; second, as a happy distraction from the horror of Maura's return. Shane still couldn't get over the fact that she had managed to escape from under his nose. Not only had he missed his chance to catch Maura and Declan, but he had also missed his chance to find Molly.

It pained Shane that she refused to give him a second chance, but he wouldn't give up. She couldn't stay angry forever, and well, they did have forever. The most painful memory Shane had was of watching Molly's body lowered into its grave. At the time, he thought there was no way to revive her headless body. It was that mistake that caused the rift between them. Maura had somehow managed to bring her back to life and poisoned Molly against him. Shane refused to lose her again. He crossed the room to where she sat and

47

extended his hand.

"Care to dance?" he asked, but she just rolled her eyes and made her way to the buffet table.

Maybe he should take Gretchen's advice and give her space to cool down. However, Shane wasn't sure just how much space would be too little. Any amount of space was too much in Shane's opinion. Shane hoped Claude had more luck with Gretchen than he had with Molly.

CHAPTER 4

The last person Gretchen expected to see at her door in the morning was Claude. He leaned against the door jamb in that sexy, lazy way of his that made her want to swoon. Wearing a sheepish grin, he offered her a mug of blood.

"What do you want?" She eyed the mug suspiciously but didn't take it.

"Just bringing you breakfast, and I wanted to apologize. I know I've been coming on rather strong, and I don't want to make things more complicated for you."

Gretchen was shocked. This was not what she had expected from him.

"I'm glad you are starting to see the light." She smiled and did a little dance in her head.

"I'm not saying I'm going to stop. Even if I could, I'm not sure that's something either of us would be happy with."

Her inner celebration stopped, and she frowned at him.

"I will admit that there is considerable lust between us, but will you at least tone it down a little?"

She could compromise if he could. She hated

admitting that he was right about her wanting him, but it wasn't like she could hide her attraction either way.

"Do you want a real answer?" His eyes slid slowly over her body making her squirm.

Only Claude could make her feel so hot and vulnerable with just a look. He took a step closer bringing the cup to her lips. They stared into each other's eyes as she drank. His hazel eyes molten with desire as he watched her swallow. Only when there was nothing left did he pull the mug away.

Gretchen felt a small drop of blood resting on her lip, but before she could lick it away, Claude reached up and ran his thumb across her lip. Gretchen held her breath as his finger lingered a moment before she tilted her head forward, bringing it into her mouth. She sucked the last drop away.

"You're playing with fire," he growled, closing the space between them.

Before she knew it, she was in his arms, and his head bent towards hers. Maybe she had taken her teasing a bit too far. She turned her head, shrinking away from him, and he immediately released her.

Get a grip, Gretch!

"I—I'll see you at training," she stammered refusing to look at him. Gretchen wasn't sure if she was angrier with herself or Claude.

He didn't say anything as he stalked away.

***

Claude watched as Gretchen positioned herself in front of her target. Her stance was all wrong. Her legs were too far apart, and her shoulders were way too stiff. He winced as she pulled back on the bow string. It was way too much.

He wasn't surprised when the arrow sailed right of the target, firmly embedding in the concrete wall behind it. Apparently, she hadn't retained any of the information from their last class.

Either that or she was still upset about earlier. Claude hoped it wasn't the latter. She had seemed tense from the start when he had brought her breakfast and apologized to her. Then things had gotten a little out of hand. He'd moved too quickly and now was back at square one. If it had been that much of a problem, she could have declined training today, but instead she was here with him, alone in the back garden.

They had initially had lessons in the courtyard, but Gretchen's lack of control and the wedding had moved them out to the back of the garden. With the way Gretchen was shooting today, it was a much safer situation, for others at least. He, on the other hand, was simultaneously in danger of being shot and mauled.

The mauling he wouldn't mind. Claude placed his hand on the small of Gretchen's back, and she stiffened under his touch. It was Xander who had suggested he teach Gretchen archery. It was a good way for her to gauge her strength and get used to the new way her eyes could focus in on things.

"Okay, now try to aim at the center."

"I was aiming at the center."

"Then, should we go back to the basics?"

Gretchen glared at him, her lips pressed into a thin line, but she didn't say anything.

Progress, she's still angry, but her silence means I haven't completely ruined my chances.

Claude smiled to himself and pressed his body closer to her back, lining up their bodies. He reached for the bow in her hands. Helping to adjust her position, he forced himself to stay focused on the task at hand and not on how good she felt against him. With Gretchen now in the proper stance, he leaned closer to whisper in her ear.

He couldn't help it. What kind of man would he be if he didn't use the situation to his advantage? His gaze fell to her neck, where he knew a thick scar still remained even despite her change. He knew Gretchen was a little self-conscious of it since she wore turtlenecks every day, even on a warm afternoon like this one.

"Carefully now." His manhood hardened as he felt her slight shiver.

❈❈❈

Gretchen fought the shudder working its way through her body. Having him pressed against her this way was hazardous to her already unsteady nerves. Doing her best to ignore the sexual tension between them she slowly pulled back.

She bit her lip to keep from moaning as Claude's hand made its way up her body to stop her in the correct position. The warmth of his hand over hers was bad enough. She almost swooned when it returned to her hip.

"That's it, now release."

His voice, low and sultry, in her ear was almost too much. She didn't so much as release her hold on the bow as she did lose all the strength in her body. It was all she could do not to melt into him.

"Bulls eye!"

She vaguely registered his words as he spun her into his arms and hugged her tightly against him. Her muddled brain refused to work properly. Should she push him away or just give in to her body's urgings? She looked up into his eyes, and it was as if the world around them didn't exist. It was just the two of them trapped in a fog of lust.

She dropped her bow, arms coming up to circle around his neck. His head bent towards hers; lips slightly parted for a kiss. She tilted her head up to meet him.

"It's about time," a voice said breaking them from the moment.

Gretchen turned to find Xander and Cat standing a few feet away dressed in their fencing costumes, but missing their rapiers. They usually used the courtyard for their training, but Gretchen doubted they had come to this secluded corner of the gardens to fence. It was Xander who had spoken, and Cat was glaring up at him.

Gretchen immediately pushed away from Claude. She ran down the path back to the house and up to her room. She was so embarrassed. How could she have let that happen? No, this wasn't her fault. It was all Claude's doing. Claude had done it again; he'd used her body's reaction against her.

Feeling overwhelmed by her warring emotions, Gretchen took a long hot shower before throwing herself into reading one of Felix's papers on the MacDonald Estate. She had read them all before, but now, knowing the truth, they read like fiction novels. Instead of a charming Scottish estate it was more Dracula's castle. Its walls held the dark secrets of murder, slavery, and torture.

In a way, reading them again was her way of grieving him. He had been a good friend to her. She had been horrible not to see what was going on when he had disappeared. Even as she tried to focus on other things, her mind still kept drifting back to Claude.

She was glad he had left her alone after their dance, but as soon as she'd seen him this evening he hadn't relented. He'd brought her breakfast in bed and insisted on helping her adjust to her new abilities. When he was acting as a teacher, Claude wasn't all that bad. Until today, he had been focused on the task at hand and not tempting her to jump him. It made him seem almost human, and her heart melted to him a little. Of course, that had been the problem all along. She couldn't afford for her heart to become a puddle for him.

"Don't let him wear you down," Molly said intruding on Gretchen's thoughts.

Gretchen started. She had been too caught up in her own head to notice that Molly had entered her room. Gretchen was grateful for both the intrusion and the advice.

"No worries, Claude is not even close to what I want."

Molly rolled her eyes, chomping loudly on a piece of gum. It was a recent habit of hers, ever since Shane had let it slip that it was a major pet peeve of his.

"I said not to let him wear you down, not lie to yourself. It will only be easier for him if you try to deny what you're feeling. It's better to accept it. That way you will be better prepared to manage your feelings around him."

"Is that what you do with Shane?"

Gretchen knew she was playing with fire, but her tumultuous mood wouldn't let her care.

"Our situation is different."

Gretchen could see Molly mentally shutting down. It happened any time someone brought up Shane around her. Gretchen knew that there was still love between them. It was obvious in the way they acted around each other. You couldn't possibly hate someone that much if there wasn't already intense emotion. It was one of the things that scared her most about Claude. She might not love him, but she had a serious crush. It was just her luck that the first man she was attracted to in years was someone she had no business liking. Yes, Claude had saved her life by turning her instead of letting her die in the forest, but that didn't mean she should give him her heart.

"Claude may not have betrayed me, but he has other characteristics that make him unacceptable," Gretchen said hoping to end the conversation soon.

It wasn't that she didn't want to talk with Molly. Claude was a non-topic for Gretchen. It was no secret that Claude was a womanizer. No matter how different he acted around her, she wouldn't be drawn in. That was exactly what had gotten her in trouble the last time. The reason she'd taken the internship with Felix and ran away to Scotland in the first place. That should have been the first warning, when Justin began making special efforts to talk to her and lure her away from friends.

He had invited her out several times before that party, but she had always refused; partially because Gina had already staked her claim, and partially because she hadn't been interested in being yet another conquest to him. That's exactly what she hadn't wanted, and exactly what she had become, just another of Justin's conquests. Just thinking of it made Gretchen's resolve harden against Claude. There was no way she would ever be conquered again. Her next partner would be just that, a partner. There would be equal surrender.

"If assholes could fly this place would be an airport," Molly huffed, twisting a strand of her hair, "This isn't getting either of us anywhere. Do you want to be bad and sneak out for ice cream? I'm sure you can still taste that now, right?"

"Are you sure we can get away with it?"

"Why not? Xander and Cat are in their own little love

bubble. Claude is out already and Shane. Well, to be honest, he's probably in a drugged stupor."

"Drugged stupor?"

"Never mind, let's just go," Molly said, grabbing Gretchen's hand and dragging her to the door.

Gretchen was surprised how easy it had been to leave. She hadn't exactly tried it before, but the way the men of the house talked about security, Gretchen had been sure there was an entire private army waiting for any sign of unauthorized movement. Instead, Molly had gotten into one of the three sleek, black sports cars parked out front, and they had driven past both guard stations with no issue. Gretchen hadn't thought about leaving the mansion before. The threat of Maura looming and adjusting to life as a Vampire had kept her mind occupied enough not to wonder too much about what lay beyond the walls of the mansion.

They passed two ice cream shops before Molly pulled into the parking lot of one on the other side of town. Gretchen didn't question Molly's motives for choosing this particular one, but she was sure it was probably the furthest one from the house. It was a little weird for Gretchen to be out in America again. She hadn't realized just how much she had changed during her stay in Scotland. They went to the counter and ordered their ice cream before seating themselves in a window booth. Molly apparently didn't feel the need to hide out.

"I never realized how suffocating being in that house was until now," Gretchen said after savoring her first bite of chocolate ice cream.

It wasn't like they didn't have ice cream at the house, but somehow being out here instead of there made it ten times better. Almost as if her sense of taste was increasing instead of decreasing as it had been the past few months.

"You are totally right."

"I understand the boys being on red alert because of Maura, but seriously, I have nothing to do with that mess. As soon as I learn how to manage this whole Vamp thing, I'm leaving." Gretchen scooped up another spoonful of her dessert.

"Maura won't be looking for me either. She has already had her fill of me. As soon as I find a decent job, I'm leaving too."

"You will definitely be gone before I will. I mean look at Cat, she's had five years of knowing about vampires then becoming one herself and she is still dealing with things."

Molly scrunched up her face.

"That's because the boys shelter her too much. I've had less time to adjust then she has, and I was doing perfectly well before I realized Maura and Declan were insane."

"I know you spent a lot of time with Declan, but I can't imagine him being a normal human being," Gretchen pondered aloud.

"Oh, he wasn't, but I owed him my life." Molly shrugged.

"That's how I feel about Claude. I don't know if this crush is more Stockholm syndrome than anything real."

"Exactly, now that you realize what it is. It will be much easier for you to ignore him."

"You make it sound so easy."

"Well, if you really think it's Stockholm syndrome, then you should move out with me. I can help you deal with your change, and you can keep me company. One thing about being a Vamp is the loneliness. It's what drew Shane out the night we met."

"I don't need any more reassurance. I'm sure that's

what this is."

"Then it's settled. As soon as I can find a job and a place, we'll blow that popsicle stand," Molly said, a smile on her face.

It was the first time Gretchen had seen Molly smile, and it made Gretchen smile as well. They were in this together now. It was only a matter of time before they wouldn't have to worry about Claude or Shane ever again. A part of Gretchen felt relieved, but the other felt sorry for Shane. Although she understood the need for independence, Gretchen was also certain that Molly and Shane were soulmates.

❊❊❊

Smiling to himself, Claude strolled through the garden to the shed where they stored their practice equipment when it wasn't in use. He doubted Gretchen would be available for archery lessons again after the scene back there. If only Xander and Cat had kept their honeymoon in the bedroom, the things that could have and should have happened between Gretchen and himself.

His tongue ran over his bottom lip; he was still able to taste her green apple flavored lip balm. It was one of her pleasant little quirks. Most women went for the cliché cherry, but not Gretchen. The sweet yet tart flavor suited her perfectly. She was all girl next door until you got under her skin.

"Deny it all you want darling, but you're mine," he said out loud, mentally congratulating himself for finding a crack in her defenses.

Just thinking about her different layers had Claude mentally stripping her out of that damned turtle neck and jeans she was so fond of wearing. Claude was all for progress, but women in pants were the worst. He preferred them in dresses and skirts, especially the modern versions of such garments. They were perfect for easy access. Stumbling on a crack in the path, his body tipped forward making his sunglasses slip from his face.

His attention now firmly back to the task at hand, he picked up his pace. He could daydream later. Right now, he needed to finish putting away their gear. That didn't mean that as soon as he was finished, he wouldn't go straight to Gretchen room and persuade her to pick things up where they were so rudely interrupted.

"What in the hell?" he muttered when he opened door to the equipment shed.

It was a complete mess inside, which was unusual. Xander was a stickler for order, and he would never stand for such disrespectful treatment of his equipment. Almost nothing was in its correct place. Even more unusual, there wasn't a single trace, other than the mess, that anyone had been to the shed since he had arrived earlier to retrieve the equipment needed for today's lesson.

The only person who didn't leave any trace of their presence was Molly. You could sense her physical presence, but that was it. Nothing about her lingered in her absence, it was a trick that even Maura hadn't mastered.

"That red-headed she-devil," he cursed.

It bugged him just how little they knew regarding the details of how she was turned. By all rights, she had been dead, decapitated, with no way of coming back to life. Claude had even attended her funeral with Shane and Cat; he'd seen her body lowered into a proper grave. It still gave him the creeps every time he saw her.

"Soulless, man-hating witch," he continued.

Molly appeared to be human. Her skin still held color, her touch was human warm, and even her sense of taste remained the same, if her gusto for eating real food was to be believed. The only thing that signified her change was, well, she had come back from the dead, had fangs, needed to drink blood to survive, and like the rest of them preferred to live a mostly nocturnal life.

"What the hell happened here?" a voice said from behind him.

Claude turned to see Xander standing in the doorway, his jaw set in anger. He was surprised Cat wasn't attached to Xander's hip, like they had been ever since the incident at MacDonald Estate.

"It was like this when I got here. There's no trace of anyone though," he replied, earning an incredulous look from Xander.

He watched Xander study the scene and come to the same conclusion he had earlier.

"I think it's time we had another talk with Cat and Shane about Molly," Xander said, before storming off towards the house.

As much as Claude would love to see Molly given the boot, this wasn't going to be good. Xander's temper could very well get them all in a world of trouble. There was too much at stake to make any rash decisions. Besides, they had already decided that keeping Molly close was better than having her vulnerable to Maura again. At least having her at the mansion, they could keep an eye on her and make sure she wasn't helping Maura in her plans for revenge.

He tossed down the equipment still in his hand and went after Xander. At the very least, he could calm him down before he faced off with those two. Shane was usually pretty timid, but Molly was his mate, and he would kill for her. Molly was also Cat's best friend, and those two had been virtually inseparable since Molly's surprise return. How Cat had ever forgiven Molly for threatening her life, Claude had no idea, but he did know that Cat was fiercely protective of her anyway. There wouldn't have even been a wedding if Xander hadn't relented on having Molly stay.

"Xander! Let's discuss this before you go and make our lives worse." Claude grabbed Xander's arm. He barely managed to stop him before he'd made it to the study where they usually had important discussions.

"The sooner she is gone, the safer everyone will be." Xander snatched his arm away.

"Maybe, or she could run and tell Maura all about our little set up. Not to mention, your new wife will surely make the rest of your life a living hell if you force Molly to leave." Claude waited for his friend to relax his aggressive stance.

"She doesn't even want to be here," Xander sighed and rubbed at his brow. The stress of the situation apparent in the defeated slump of his shoulders.

"Yeah, but Cat, and more importantly Shane, need her to be here. I don't know about you, but between Cat's temper and Shane's bad romance, it's the only option that guarantees any peace at the moment."

"We need to find Maura. It goes against everything inside me to wait for her next attack."

"I'll get right on it. She will need blood, and I'm sure she is somewhere close. If Molly knew where to find us, it makes sense that she got that information from Maura or Declan. All I have to do is look for a blood trail."

"Fine. We will leave Molly for now, and tomorrow night we start our hunt."

Xander turned away from the door to the study and headed the opposite direction towards his room.

"Tomorrow night, I'll be ready," Shane's weak, gravelly voice said catching Claude completely off guard.

Claude looked back to see Shane in the doorway. It was a shame in his pre-Vampire life that Shane had been a pacifist because he would have made one hell of a spook.

"I think you should sit tomorrow night out." Claude took note of Shane's thin almost sickly frame.

With the advanced healing ability that Vampirism afforded, it took a lot of damage to achieve such a gaunt look. The sad part, it was still better then how he was before they had found out Molly was alive. At least now he had hope that Shane would start to turn himself around. Claude was worried about his friend and not just his physical health. In all honesty, with Shane's mental state, he would be more of a liability than an asset in any dangerous situation they would come across.

"I'm going with you." The determination set in Shane's eyes was only weakened by their sunken, hollow appearance.

"It's better if you stay here, in case Maura makes a move on this place."

"She won't. That isn't her way, Maura doesn't come to you. You go to her."

Shane had a point, but they didn't have the luxury to assume that things hadn't changed.

"Let's discuss this tomorrow."

"No, we will discuss it now. I know what you all think, that I'm too fragile, but I'm not. I'm ready and more than willing to take my part in destroying that bitch. I won't just stand on the sidelines this time."

"Alright, all three of us will go tomorrow." Claude hated to give in, but ultimately, Shane would be staying. There was no way Xander would allow him to come, and right now Claude didn't have the patience to continue to argue with him.

Shane eyed him warily but moved in his slow, halting gait towards his section of the house.

Claude sighed with relief, "Disaster averted."

For a brief moment, he contemplated returning to the shed to fix the disaster that was still there, but then he thought about Gretchen, alone in her room, and changed his mind. He took the stairs two at a time and didn't even bother knocking on her room door before flinging it open.

"Now where were we," he announced to an empty room.

His cocky smirk faltered as he realized he was all alone. Maybe she was with Cat and Molly in the theater room. The girls liked to congregate there and have little girl chats. He left the room and walked back down the stairs. The theater room was in Shane's domain, but he wasn't as territorial about it as the rest of his space. When he saw that it was empty as well, a brief moment of panic overtook him before he sprinted down the hall, past the study, and to the kitchen.

He skidded to a halt as he encountered a thong wearing Xander raiding the fridge. Cat obviously wasn't with the girls. Xander was kind of a prude, so only the urgency of pending sex would have him so exposed in any area of the house outside of his room.

"She's gone!" he blurted, startling Xander and causing him to drop the bowl of grapes he'd been holding.

"Who's gone?" Xander bent over to clean up the newly made mess while trying to shield his partially naked body from Claude.

"Gretchen, she isn't in her room, and she isn't in the theater. She's obviously not with Cat." Claude rambled, and Xander had the nerve to burst into a fit of laughter.

"Man, you have got it bad. This is truly amusing. She could be in Molly's room or still in the gardens. There are lots of places on this property she could be."

"She's not that close to Molly, and she rarely leaves her room."

"Just go ask Molly."

"Yeah right. Like Molly would even open her door for me."

"I'd love to help you, but I'm kind of busy. Just let the girl have some space."

Claude threw his hands up in defeat and headed out to the garden. Something just wasn't right about this, and it wasn't the fact that he'd just seen Xander in a thong.

❈❈❈

Going out for ice cream had been fun, but for Gretchen, going back to the mansion was nerve racking. It almost felt like the times she'd snuck home well after curfew as a teen. The tension building in her shoulders was the same at least.

"Oh, don't be so tense. I doubt anyone has even noticed. I do this all the time," Molly said, obviously amused by the situation.

Gretchen was the first to admit she knew close to nothing about Molly, but her experience with her today was a far cry from the gullible, good girl the others had described her as. This Molly had a dark side that Gretchen wasn't entirely sure had anything to do with her drama with Shane. Still, Gretchen was inclined to trust her. Who wouldn't be changed by the trauma she'd been through? It made Gretchen's turning seem tame. At least, Gretchen had kept her head. Molly

64

wasn't physically scarred by her ordeal, but the mental scars had to be much deeper.

"Where do you go? I mean; it must be hard trying to avoid places you used to frequent."

"Oh, here and there. I hate being cooped up for so long, and it's not like those boys are the only Vamps in town, as much as they like to act like they are."

"Wait, there's more of us?"

"Of course, there are, it's not like that bitch Maura is the only ancient Vamp. Though, I have learned she is the oldest as far as anyone knows. She is one serious mental case, so the others tend to steer clear of anyone associated with her."

"So, how did you get to know them?"

"They found me. How else do you think I got here all the way from Scotland with no money and no plan? They saw how ragged and desperate I was and being female, they knew I couldn't possibly be in league with her."

"I still find it weird how you and Maura were at MacDonald Estate that the whole time, and I had no idea."

"Well, you didn't exactly come inside often, and that place has a lot more secrets than any one person could ever know."

"Wait, so if there are others, and you are friendly with them, why are you still at the mansion?"

"Hmmm—mansion or run-down basement living, which would you choose? Other Vampires are more nomadic. They don't stick around and rely on bagged blood like the boys do, so their accommodations aren't as important to them."

"I guess I've read too many Vampire novels then."

"Not all of them are like that either. I've been told in the major cities like Los Angeles and San Francisco there are more civilized Vamps with major infrastructures and class systems and all that, but Maura is my sire, so I would probably be killed on the spot."

"I know you don't like to talk about it, but how exactly did Maura sire you? I mean, from what the others said, it should have been impossible, you know, the whole missing a head thing."

"You ask a lot of questions, you know that?" Molly said, shaking her head.

"Sorry, my curiosity is kind of a curse."

"You got that straight. Curiosity killed the cat isn't just a saying in your case."

Her words sent a chill down Gretchen's spine, and even the cheerful grin she flashed didn't help. Molly was right; it had been curiosity that brought her to Scotland, curiosity that hadn't let her drop the issue of Felix's disappearance, and curiosity that led her away from the group when Declan wanted to talk.

Maybe it was time Gretchen be a little less curious. It surely hadn't done her many favors in the past. Despite the millions of questions running through her head, Gretchen kept quiet. They spent the rest of the ride back to the mansion in virtual silence.

CHAPTER 5

She wasn't in the garden. Claude searched every inch of it three times before checking her room again, then the theater, and the kitchen twice more. He'd even interrupted Xander and Cat's little love fest to ask if Cat had any idea where else she could be. Xander had nearly ripped his head off, but it had been worth it. Claude was now 100% sure Gretchen was not on the grounds thanks to the security guard at the gate.

"Mr. Smith's car is the only one to pass through the gates today, about an hour ago." The guard checked the log sheet in front of him.

"Mr. Smith hasn't left the grounds all day." Claude couldn't hold back the edge in his voice.

"It was the red-headed woman, driving. She's been using Mr. Smith's car for a while now, so I recognized her. She is usually alone but had another female with her this time. I thought it might be Mrs. Smith."

"Thank you, inform me when they come back." Claude stalked away from the security booth, hands clenched into fists at his side. It had taken all his restraint not to kill the man for letting them off the property, but this particular guard had been with them longer than any of the others. There was something to be said for his loyalty even if he was possibly the worst guard in the world. Okay, maybe not the worst, but at the moment that's how Claude saw it.

They had beefed up security, but Molly had taken Xander's car, so there was no reason for the man to question its comings and goings. At least now they knew Molly was definitely up to something, he just prayed that kidnapping Gretchen wasn't part of that plan. Xander wasn't going to be happy about a second intrusion, but this new information was too crucial to keep from him.

"Sorry Cat, but this is too much. We can't trust her any longer," Claude argued for the fifth time in ten minutes. He'd interrupted the happy couple in their coital bliss, so of course Cat had insisted on joining their discussion in the study.

"She was held hostage for two years! Who cares if she wants to get out every once in a while?"

"She stole Xander's keys!"

"She didn't steal them. I gave her my set since I wasn't going to be using them."

"You what!" Xander chimed in, glaring at his wife.

"I gave her the keys. I know just as well as you do that she doesn't feel comfortable here. I gave her the keys so she could go to job interviews and things." Cat rubbed her temples with her fingers.

"And give the layout of the mansion and its security to Maura," Xander countered, and Cat rolled her eyes.

"Molly has nothing to do with Maura anymore!"

"How do you know that for sure?"

"She's my best friend. I trust her."

"She tried to kill you!" Xander roared. His hands clenched firmly at his sides. Xander was typically the pillar of restraint, but he was easily brought to shaking rages when it came to Cat.

"No, that was your creepy shadow girlfriend. The spell Maura gave to Molly would only have scared me, but your stupid girlfriend made it real so she could transfer the necklace holding Maura's power to me. Don't blame Molly for that."

"What? Shadow girlfriend? Xander, please tell me you know what she's talking about?" Claude shook his head as he took in Xander's equally perplexed look.

Cat sighed and flopped down on the couch. Adjusting her robe so it modestly covered her long brown legs. Cat was a true ebony goddess, but Claude had never seen her in a sexual way. It had taken a lot to get them to the point of friendship to begin with. She was perfectly Xander's opposite and his mate.

"I meant to tell you before, but I've been getting visits from a shadow figure that I think is Rachel, Xander's ex-girlfriend."

"Like dreams?" Xander sat next to his wife. Taking her into his arms, a worried look on his face.

"No, she actually appears. It's happened twice now. The first time was while you were all in Scotland looking for Felix. She told me that you were all in danger, and she showed me things about your past with Maura. She also explained to me about the necklace. Maura got the necklace somehow and used it to hold her dark magic.

Without it, she is weaker, but she can't be destroyed until the dark magic is. The second visit was the day before our wedding. I wasn't able to sleep, so I went to the courtyard, and she came to me again. This time she told me that in order to destroy the magic and Maura, Shane and Claude had to find true love."

Claude rolled his eyes. "I think Shane might have slipped you something. How in the world will that help us defeat Maura?"

"Look, I think it's crazy too, but I have no reason to

doubt The Shadow."

"How do you even know this shadow is Rachel? It could be something Maura's cooked up to distract us," Xander said, pulling Cat into his arms.

"It's hard to explain. Believe me or don't, but I don't get a bad vibe from The Shadow, so I trust it."

"So I have to fall in love?"

"And have it reciprocated, fairy tale love," Cat laughed.

"Then we are surely screwed," Xander said, holding his wife tighter.

"Alright, alright, but back to the matter at hand. Where the hell would Molly take Gretchen?" Claude waved his hand in the air as if to hurry Cat along.

"Probably for ice cream."

"We have ice cream here." Claude was perplexed.

"Not the point." Cat stood and patted Claude on the shoulder before leaving the room with Xander in tow.

"This is insane," Claude huffed before he began to pace.

This was all some sick joke. Maura had to be behind this somehow. How could his falling in love have anything to do with destroying Maura? If anything, it would destroy him first. And where the hell were those crazy women? The longer they were gone, the more upset he got.

Claude went to wait in Gretchen's room first, but after thirty minutes he moved to pacing by the entry hall, until finally he was outside sitting on the front step, waiting. His ears perked up at the first sounds of crunching gravel, and when the car pulled up his heart started to race, well, beat normally if compared to a human's.

When Gretchen stepped out of the car he had so much he wanted to say, but all he could do was stand there and glare at her.

"I think I'll skip this lover's quarrel." Molly pushed passed Claude on her way inside leaving him alone with Gretchen.

Claude let her go. She would get what was coming to her later, right now all that mattered was Gretchen. She was back, she was safe, and she was never leaving again.

"I don't have anything to say to you," Gretchen said, and tried to move around him, but he grabbed her and hauled her up tight against his body.

"Good," Claude hissed and crushed his lips to hers. He'd meant to yell at her, to express to her just how stupid of a risk she had taken by leaving the mansion, but when he'd seen her, he'd been flooded with relief and an urgency to express a whole different set of feelings to her.

❈❈❈

Gretchen wanted to be angry that he had waited for her, but he'd looked so cute sitting on the front step, almost like a puppy welcoming their owner home after a long trip. Then he'd acted all bull-headed male, reminding her exactly why she wanted to leave in the first place.

Seriously? Blocking the door like he was some bouncer at a club!

She'd thought she could just walk right by like Molly had, but of course, she was wrong. He'd swept her off her feet, caveman style and was currently reminding her body just how long it had been sexually dormant.

His kiss may lack the finesse of the last, but it was definitely scorching her from the inside out. At first just an angry mash of lips that had her ready to slap him silly, but her baser instincts kicked into gear before her brain could signal for any prohibitive actions. Instead, she found herself reaching up to stroke his muscled chest and neck, it was the only real movement possible as his vice like grip held her not only off the ground, but impossibly close to his slim, muscular frame.

Gretchen tried not to think of the implications of their actions, especially as he carried her over the threshold and up to his room. She only wanted to feel as he laid her gently on his bed. She watched as he made quick work of his clothing. It was no seductive strip tease, just an efficient shucking of clothing, but the reveal of his manhood didn't need any extra trapping to get her worked up. He was beautiful, long, but not outrageously so, with enough girth to make sure she felt every inch.

As he moved closer, her brain started working again. Screaming warning after warning, but it was too late. Things had gone too far and maybe, just maybe, she needed to give in. Get him out of her system, let him get her out of his system, and then this stupid game of theirs could end. Her heart had nothing to do with this. It was just flesh against flesh, or at least it would be once she joined him in the birthday suit club.

She forced her gaze up to his eyes as she began to disrobe. Her fingers desperately fumbling with the button on her jeans. Any thought she had of playing the seductress was dashed by her clumsiness and Claude's impatience. He pushed her hand away and skillfully disrobed her. Another reminder of just how experienced he was in these matters.

She closed her eyes as Claude pressed soft kisses to her exposed breasts, his hands drifting downward to rub gently at her sex. Reveling in the excitement of being manipulated by something not battery operated for the first time in ages, she arched her back, lifting her hips and encouraging to explore her body deeper.

With a groan he complied, sliding one finger inside her she hissed at the slight intrusion. She had expected to be a little tight, but not that much. Claude moved his kisses from her breasts to her neck as he gently stroked her, patiently letting her body adjust, but the sense of urgency was still there, tightly coiled in her belly.

"Just fuck me already," she gasped, and he chuckled.

"No," he said, slowing the already leisurely pace of his fingers.

"No?"

"If this is to be my only chance, I plan to savor it."

Gretchen didn't know whether to scream in frustration or cheer in anticipation. Sex with Claude was bound to be good, but she wasn't sure she could keep her feelings out of it if he took his time with her. He was still stroking her, priming her body for his throbbing erection. She knew he wanted her just as much as she wanted him. She wasn't going to give him another time.

"You have all of tonight to savor, but now I just need release."

He scowled at her for a moment before using his thumb to press firmly on her clit while he stroked inside of her with his other fingers. Her inner muscles began to quiver, and her hands fisted in the sheets as she fought the impending orgasm. Yes, she had wanted it, but not like this. Claude shifted above her, his erection pressed against her inner thigh.

Was he going to give her what she wanted, or was he just being a tease? Her body wasn't going to wait for an answer. She cried out as pleasure began to concentrate at her core. There was no stopping it as it snowballed and exploded, sending waves of satisfaction through her. Claude kissed her, claiming her mouth until the last spasms subsided.

"That wasn't exactly what I had in mind," she managed and he frowned, removing his fingers from inside of her. He rolled off of her and sat at the edge of the bed. The tension in the room went from sexually charged to positively icy in no time.

"I can't give you what you want."

"Can't or won't because he definitely looks up to the task," she said gesturing at his still rigid flesh.

This was exactly what Gretchen had wanted to avoid. She didn't understand why he was acting this way.

Claude cupped her face with his hands, forcing him to meet his serious gaze. "I won't be used."

There was something in his eyes that hinted at some deep pain, but for the life of her Gretchen couldn't get passed her anger to ask about it.

"What? You won't be used? If that isn't the most hypocritical load of crap!"

Fire blazed in the glare he shot her, but it was nothing compared to the inferno raging inside of her. She grabbed her clothes and stormed from the room, not trusting herself to keep her temper in check. The whole situation had been a major mistake.

She stomped down the hall, not caring that she was naked. It was doubtful anyone would see on the short trip to her room. Once in her room, the anger began to subside only to be replaced by embarrassment and a million questions.

CHAPTER 6

Declan scanned the club again for the perfect one. It was getting late so the girls were getting drunker and more desperate to leave with someone, anyone. It was that kind of girl that Declan needed. One that was young and pretty, but ultimately so insecure and wasted, he didn't have to use an ounce of charm.

Then he spotted her, curly brown hair and freckles.

Just like that bitch, Gretchen.

Declan would get to her one of these days, but until then he satisfied himself by sending her look-a-likes to be slaughtered by Maura. He made his way across the room, syrupy girl drink in hand. She smiled seductively at him as she accepted it.

"I've been watching you." Declan ran a finger down her arm, and she giggled.

"Really?"

She played shy, but the way she pressed her body into his, Declan knew it was purely an act.

"Let's get out of here." He took her hand. She didn't protest as he led her out of the bar and away from the crowd at the door.

She tottered on her too tall heels like one of those

weighted children's toys. With her level of intoxication, it was a feat in itself that she managed to stay upright. Still she clung to him like he was her own personal life preserver. Stupid cunt.

"Where are we going?" The girl giggled as Declan dragged her into the dark alley behind the bar.

"Disneyland," Declan sneered. He was not in a good mood, not only had he not been laid in several months, but he was starved.

Maura had made it perfectly clear that her feeding schedule was more important than his which made it really hard for him to maintain the energy he needed. His fangs burned with need as the girl pressed her body closer to his. He could feel her pulse from his grip on her wrist. It was strong and lively, and for a moment he almost lost his control.

I could have this one for myself and get another girl for Maura just like that.

Just as the thought crossed his mind, a sharp pain ran through his entire body making him flinch. It was the same pain that nearly crippled him the last time he had tried to defy Maura's orders. She was getting stronger, and he was getting weaker. At this rate, there was no way he could get out from under her.

At least he wasn't the only one. In the last city they had picked up two new members, Axel and Rod, brothers. Axel wasn't the brightest guy, but what he lacked in intellect he made up for in muscle. He was also quite the sexual deviant which meant Maura denied Declan the only perk left in this gig.

Rodney, or Rod as he liked to be called, could at least hold a decent conversation without resorting to manly posturing and fart jokes. He wasn't good looking enough to handle the ladies, but he was a fast talker and proved himself capable of talking his way in and out situations that Declan had no idea how to even conceptualize.

Declan helped the feeder fish back onto her feet. His involuntary muscle spasm had knocked her over.

"I guess I'm not the only tipsy one," the girl sang, blowing her putrid breath in his face.

Declan fought back the rising bile in his throat.

You deserve everything that's coming, sloppy bitch.

He managed to get her into the car at the other end of the alley. The girl didn't even notice he hadn't gotten in with her. As soon as Rod had pulled off Declan headed down the street to the next club, one more girl and then he could feed.

❊❊❊

Maura frowned at the young girl standing in front of her. This was the third girl with curly brown hair and freckles. Although Maura usually didn't care how a girl looked, as long as she was young and beautiful, this was a disturbing recurrence with Declan's acquisitions. He was still obsessing over that girl. Declan was becoming increasingly useless as time passed and her plan progressed. His days were quite literally numbered. Once Maura found a man to replace Declan's intellect then she would be rid of him.

Maura signaled for Rod to hold the girl steady.

"Wow, you're beautiful," the girl murmured as Maura got closer.

"Thanks to you darling, thanks to you," Maura whispered in the girl's ear before biting into her neck.

The girl had been ready to pass out by the time she had been brought to Maura, so she had no fight to her. That ruined Maura's fun, so she drained her quickly before sending Rod to dispose of the body.

"Make sure the next girl isn't half dead when she gets here," Maura ordered as he gathered the body up to leave.

Maura went back to her room where Axel was waiting for her. He was positioned exactly the way she had left him. His arms were tied behind his back and attached to a chain hanging from the ceiling. It was short enough that his body weight strained his shoulders but just long enough that his toes could reach the floor. His chest and thighs were covered with angry red streaks where the barbs of her whip had torn at his flesh.

Thanks to his Vampiric healing abilities they were no longer bleeding, but they would be soon. Maura retrieved her whip, ripping it out of his anus where she had shoved it earlier. He flinched but didn't make a sound. He was abiding by her rules. She didn't want to hear his pleasure only his pain.

CHAPTER 7

Gretchen woke up gasping for air. Her hands flew to her neck, reaching for the invisible hands that had been there a few minutes before in her dream. She could feel that familiar edge of a building panic attack tingling through her body. She sat up and shook her head trying, and failing, to clear her thoughts. Taking a quick look around the room she was in, Gretchen forced herself to calm down.

She was as safe as she could possibly be in a house full of Vampires. Gretchen had a hard time coming to terms with being one now herself. She had always prided herself on being adaptable, but after several months as a Vampire, she was still dealing with her new circumstances.

The heightened senses weren't what she had expected, and more often than not, led to massive headaches. Even now, in the dead of the night, she could see everything as though it were broad daylight. The additional strength was something she also struggled with, especially around Claude, who always managed to get a rise out of her. Molly and Cat had gotten into the habit of removing anything valuable or possibly dangerous from her hands before he came into a room with her. She'd only just begun to be able to control herself around him. At least until last night.

Thinking about what could have happened that night made her angry all over again. He was such an asshole, and now she had no idea how she would be able to be around him. She only hoped today would be less eventful, but it was very unlikely. There was sure to be some discussion about her and Molly leaving the mansion. Gretchen snuggled deeper into the covers before closing her eyes again. She needed more sleep if she was going to be cordial to Claude later.

It was only a few moments before she was throwing the covers off of herself. Her mind was racing with all the "what ifs", and she wasn't willing to go down that rabbit hole again. She got up and grabbed her robe. It wasn't particularly cold, but the chill from her dream still hadn't left her. She paced her room for a moment before her senses picked up a noise from in the hall.

Curious and ready for any distraction, Gretchen opened her bedroom door a crack and took a peek. At first, she didn't see anything, but as she began to close the door, a shadowy figure appeared. Startled, Gretchen fell back and screamed. The shadow stood above her, silently, but not menacingly. Even still, she was paralyzed with fear.

"You will have more to fear outside of these walls," The Shadow said, and then disappeared right before Claude burst into the room followed shortly by Xander and Shane.

"What happened?" Claude demanded, but there was a genuine glint of worry in his eyes as he studied her.

"It was just a dream."

She forced herself up, not wanting to show how shaken she was. She shoved her hands in the pockets of her robe to hide their trembling. Xander and Shane exchanged looks with Claude before leaving her alone with him.

"What kind of dream?"

"A bad one, obviously."

Claude crossed what little space there was between them and hugged her. She hated that his embrace was comforting.

"Don't touch me."

She pushed at him, trying to create space, but he stood unmoved by her effort. She dared to look into his eyes and for a moment was lost in their hazel depth. Claude's eyes darkened as his head bent lower as if to kiss her. She held her breath as his face approached hers. A hairs breadth away from the kiss they both so desperately wanted, a brief flash of regret crossed his face before it settled into a stone mask. He released her and took a step back. The absence of his warmth was more distressing than she wanted to admit, even to herself.

"Just tell me about your dream. It could have something to do with Maura. I'm sure you know about the dream Cat had before we went to Scotland."

Gretchen had heard plenty about that dream, but this hadn't been anything like that. Sure, Declan had been choking her in her dream, but The Shadow definitely appeared while she was awake. Gretchen was sure of it, and that is what truly scared her. She had to be losing her mind. The trauma of being turned so violently must have knocked a few screws loose.

"It's nothing. Just leave."

"You screamed and were on the floor. It's not nothing."

Obviously, he needed more convincing.

"I have reoccurring dreams of Declan attacking me. Are you happy now?"

"You should have told me about this before."

Gretchen rolled her eyes.

"Why? It's not exactly a mystical occurrence. I experienced a trauma. My mind is going to keep reliving it as long as the cause of the stress remains unresolved."

"Then let me help you resolve it."

"Can I leave?"

"No."

"Will you let me kill Declan?"

His hands fisted at his sides.

"I'll kill him for you."

"Will you stay out of my life?"

"I can't, even if I wanted to."

Exasperated, Gretchen flopped down on her bed.

"Can't you see that you only make things worse for me?"

He visibly flinched at her words, and Gretchen knew she had been too harsh, but she wasn't going to take it back. Not now, especially when she felt so vulnerable. An unsettling mix of unease and intense lust tickling her skin.

"Can't you see things from my perspective?" His voice was pleading. He looked like he was going to reach for her again, but his hands stayed firmly at his sides.

Gretchen refused to be swayed by the pleading in his voice. After last night, she couldn't allow any weakness around him. If only for her own sanity at that moment. She squared her shoulders and glared at him.

"I'd like to see things from your point of view, but I can't seem to get my head that far up my ass."

The muscles in Claude's jaw twitched as he glowered at her. He took a step towards her but then spun on his heel, military style, and marched from the room. He slammed the door behind him with such force that the room shook and a painting from the nearby wall fell, shattering glass everywhere.

She'd been a major bitch and he hadn't deserved it, but Gretchen didn't know how else to handle this impossible situation. Her heart ached she wanted him so badly, but everything was just so overwhelming. Gretchen reached for a nearby pillow and used it to muffle her scream of frustration. It was probably useless, but at least it wouldn't have the whole house barging into her room again.

❈❈❈

Claude paced his room angrily, unable to shake the rage burning in his gut. He had just returned from a failed hunt with Xander when they had heard Gretchen scream. Despite everything, he had rushed to her only for her to lie to him. Something other than some stupid dream had scared her. She knew it, and he knew it, stubborn as she was.

She wouldn't accept help and especially not his help. He'd never been so furious and defeated in his life. He was angry with Gretchen for pushing him away, angry with himself for allowing her to, and worst of all angry that Maura still had control over him.

His encounter with Gretchen earlier that evening had opened a wound he hadn't realized had been there. Gretchen had wanted his body, not his heart, and as much as he knew the situation was different, his time with Maura had tainted her intentions and the moment. When he got his hands on Maura, she would pay. Not only Maura, but Declan, as well. Neither would escape him, and he would show Gretchen just how far he was willing to go to prove that they had nothing to lose by being together. If she thought she could get rid of him that easy, she was dead wrong. If anything tonight had only stiffened his resolve. Claude was no knight, but winning Gretchen's heart was now his ultimate quest.

❈❈❈

"Forgive him."

Molly stilled in front of the mirror; the voice was back.

Shut up

She had first heard the disembodied voice shortly after Maura had saved her, but she'd ignored it. Only after coming to the mansion had the voice come more frequently, always goading her about Shane. Molly was forced to acknowledge it then, but she refused to answer the voice out loud.

"Forgive him."

Never

The voice wasn't in her head. When she covered her ears, the words were muffled but they always got through.

"Forgive him."

Over my dead body

She continued to fix her hair.

"You're already dead."

Molly dropped her brush and closed her eyes.

Go away

There was no answer. Molly smiled triumphantly. She was finally rid of it. She turned from the mirror and a sharp pain shot through her chest. She collapsed to the floor as the sharp shooting pain turned into burning flames covering her body. Not just a feeling, but actual flames, melting her skin before her eyes. Molly screamed, but no sound came from her gaping mouth.

"Your life will be hell without him," the voice whispered so close to her ear she could feel the shifting of the air against it.

The heat intensified as the flames spread, engulfing the room until all she could see were the angry orange and yellow peaks, dancing gaily around her melting corpse. The pain was so intense, Molly felt her mind and body give up. She slipped into darkness where she was free from the pain.

When Molly came to she was on her bed, her skin tingled, but was otherwise unharmed. She sat up and faced her mirror. Her hair and makeup were perfect. There wasn't a single mark on her face. She took a deep calming breath. Whatever crazy dream she had just woke up from, it had only hardened her resolve against staying in the mansion. Grabbing her purse, she headed for the front door. She had an appointment to keep.

Brody, one of her new Vampire friends, had invited her out for drinks. He'd called her earlier, excited about a possible business deal. Molly had agreed immediately. She'd have agreed to anything to get her out of that damned mansion and as far away from Shane as possible.

Molly released a sigh of relief as she drove past the gate guard. She had almost run into Shane as she'd made her escape. He'd been making his own nightly patrols of the mansion while Xander and Claude hunted in the city. Since Gretchen's little nightmare, everyone had been on red alert. That girl had some serious issues, and it wasn't just from having her throat torn out. Although, Molly was grateful Gretchen kept them to herself. Molly had enough drama dealing with her own crazy dreams as of late.

Molly steered Xander's car through the familiar streets of her home town. She passed the house she once shared with Cat, before the accident, and an unwelcome ache settled in her chest. Molly reached over and turned the radio up, loud dance music filling the empty space around her and forcing the pain away. She didn't want to think about the past, she only needed to focus on her future from now on. She sped up, eager to be out of the residential district and into downtown.

❈❈❈

"Why do they have to make things so complicated?"

Cat jumped as the shadow figure appeared next to the tub she was bathing in.

"I guess they don't stress privacy, where you come from," Cat replied pushing the soap bubbles to cover her naked body.

The Shadow always managed to find her alone. Even today, Xander was out hunting Maura in the city.

"You haven't done a thing to help get Claude and Shane their happily ever after."

"I'm sorry if my honeymoon wasn't reason enough not to be in my friends business."

"Destroying Maura is more important than you fornicating on every surface of the house."

Cat rolled her eyes at The Shadow.

"If it's that important, why haven't you tried talking to Molly and Gretchen? Why am I the only one graced with your presence," she sneered.

"You think I haven't? Gretchen completely shut me out and Molly, well. I literally set her on fire, and she still refuses to see the truth."

"What? You set her on fire? What the hell does that have to do with getting her to give Shane a second chance?"

"She set you on fire, and you fell into Alexander's

86

bed."

"No, he fell into mine. Anyway, that still doesn't mean it's okay to set my best friend on fire. That shit sucks, and I'm speaking from experience."

Cat grabbed her robe and stood using the robe as a shield from the shadow. As soon as she could, she would go check on Molly.

"No damage was done to your friend. At least, none that wasn't already there. I'm just here to warn you that time is running out."

Cat sighed as the shadow disappeared. Just what she needed, a deadline, on not just one, but two damn near impossible situations. Now that her relaxing bath was ruined she marched to the closet to find some clothes. She was calling a girl meeting and putting an end to this drama.

✤✤✤

"Alright you two, I've called this girl meeting because I wanted to talk about the two giant elephants in the room. Let's start with you, Gretchen," Cat said as soon as she'd corralled Molly and Gretchen into Shane's theater room.

The guys had meetings in the study. The girls had theirs in Shane's Theater room. They were the only true safe common spaces in the entire mansion. Gretchen shrunk into the leather recliner she was sitting in. Seriously, the last thing she wanted to do was talk about Claude. She might be able to avoid him in real life, but he dominated her dreams.

When she wasn't having nightmares about Declan attacking her, she was dreaming of hot, sweaty nights with Claude. If he were even half the lover he was in her imagination, then she was in serious trouble. All the more reason for her to not only avoid this discussion, but to get out of the mansion.

"I'd rather watch a movie," she grumbled.

"Me too," Molly said.

"Nope, we need to talk about this," Cat said, folding her arms over her chest. She tapped her foot like Gretchen's mother did when she was impatient.

After a few moments under Cat's intense glare, Gretchen broke.

"Fine, I give in. I gave him the opportunity to be with me on my terms, and he rejected me."

Saying it out loud gave it a finality that didn't exactly sit well with Gretchen, and judging by the look on Cat's face it didn't sit well with her either.

"What terms?"

"That's personal."

"Cat doesn't know the meaning of personal," Molly whispered to Gretchen, and they giggled.

"Since you've got so much to laugh about, why don't you tell us about Shane? Why can't you just find the same happiness you had before?"

Molly stopped laughing and glared at Cat.

"Look Cat, I know you are high on married life right now, but don't try and force us into relationships because you think it's what we need to be happy. Some women don't need male companionship to validate their existence," Molly snapped.

Gretchen winced at Molly's words and watched as the storm that was Cat began to brew. She was sure all hell was about to break loose when Xander's head popped in. Seeing the two women at odds, he came into the room grabbed his wife and carried her out over his shoulder.

"That was uh..." Gretchen didn't finish her sentence as Molly stormed out leaving her alone in the theater room.

"What set those two off now? Shane should ban you three from his theater if he doesn't want anything broken," Claude said appearing in the doorway.

He leaned against the door frame. His chest in plain sight as all he wore was a pair of swim trunks, different ones than the pair she'd seen him in the other night. He had a towel slung over his shoulder as if he were on his way to the pool instead of just coming from it.

"Girl stuff," Gretchen managed to force her gaze away from his chiseled abs.

She stood and tried to leave, but he caught her, bringing her in closer.

"Avoid me while you still can, the anticipation of you in my bed again is the ultimate foreplay," he whispered sending a shiver of arousal through her.

She looked into his eyes, seeing his need for her written across his face before he smirked and walked away. Leaving her wanting more and hating herself for it. Just a few more weeks, if things went as planned, and she would be starting a new chapter in her life. One without the sexy, but infuriating Vampire named Claude.

CHAPTER 8

"Please don't go," Shane pleaded, standing in the doorway of her room.

Startled, Molly dropped the shirt she had been folding to put in her suitcase. Molly hadn't even heard him come in as she'd been too busy packing. Too busy rushing to leave the mansion, and more importantly Shane, behind.

"There is no reason for me to stay."

Refusing to look at him, she continued to pack. The man in her doorway was not the man she thought she had loved. He was, in fact, a poor imitation, a shell of the rosy-cheeked, quick-witted man she had loved. He was the man who had abandoned her, who left her for dead and had the nerve to live in a perpetual pity party for himself.

"Is my love really not enough?"

His question tugged at her heart, but she wouldn't give in. Couldn't give in to him, not now, not ever again.

"It wasn't enough to save me. Why would it be enough to make me stay?"

Molly slammed her suitcase closed and picked up her purse. She marched over to the door and was surprised when he blocked her exit. His hand reached out and cupped her face, a familiar caress that brought tears to her eyes and a burning rage in her gut. Still she let it linger, let it burn as a reminder of their past. She moved closer, choosing just for a moment to forget the pain. She kissed him, just a soft brush of her lips over his, but he pulled her into him and deepened the kiss.

His tongue pressing into her mouth, his technique was the same, but his taste was different. Not of spicy male, but bitter, poisonous filth. She pulled away then, if she'd needed confirmation that the man in front of her was not the man she'd fallen in love with, she'd gotten it. She had been so naive, blinded by the notion of fairy tale love. Shane was poisonous not only to her, but to himself. She pushed passed him. She took the chance to look back and was relieved that he wasn't following her out.

"You better keep in touch." Cat gave Molly a hug.

"Of course, I lost my best friend once, and I have no plans on doing it again."

Cat smiled and let her go.

"If you even get a hint of where Maura is or might be, I better be your first call," Xander ground out.

"Seriously? Who else am I going to call, Ghostbusters?"

He glared at her, but Molly just smiled and slid into the driver seat of her new red sports car. Her best friend's husband wasn't sad to see her go, but Molly knew he had a hard time not knowing what her plans were.

Gretchen came bouncing out of the front door, her own small suitcase in hand. She slid into the passenger seat and Molly took off. The two of them were starting fresh, away from the mansion and hopefully away from the drama.

"I'm surprised Claude wasn't chasing you down," she

said, and Gretchen sighed.

"Only Cat knew I was leaving with you, and Claude is in town on business."

"Ah, so no messy goodbye. Good for you, making a clean break."

Gretchen smiled and looked out the window. Molly envied her, if only Shane hadn't shown up when he had, Molly would have had a clean break also.

❈❈❈

"So this is home." Gretchen eyed the downtown condo Molly had recently purchased.

It was red brick, with white shutters framing the front windows. It had a small patch of grass for its front lawn.

Molly grinned as she removed the sold sign at the edge of the front grass.

"It's not a mansion, but it's got its own charms." She headed for the door.

"Oh, I'm not complaining. I'm glad to be away from all that drama." Gretchen grabbed her bag from the back seat of Molly's car.

She followed Molly up the walkway to the front entrance. Molly opened the door and stepped inside.

"Welcome to sanctuary." Molly spread her arms wide in the small entryway.

Gretchen laughed as she stepped inside, eyeing the open layout. There was a decent sized living area and kitchen to the right, on the left was a set of stairs going up to the second floor.

"I, of course, have the master suite, but you are welcome to either the room next door or the room on the main floor. There is also a basement suite, but I'm planning to rent that to other Vamps who need a place to stay," Molly said nonchalantly as she headed up the stairs.

"I'll take the main floor room. I appreciate you letting me crash with you, but I plan on getting a job and paying rent."

"No worries. You can work with me."

"And what exactly is your work?" Gretchen was curious. Molly had been disappearing almost every night for the past few weeks, and it had put the boys on edge. She'd been very secretive about what she was doing. Cat was probably the only person who knew what had been going on.

"I own a nightclub. I had to fire the old manager, and I'm sure you would be good for the job."

Gretchen thought for a moment before smiling.

"Deal, but I don't make any promises."

"Awesome, you can start tonight," Molly said and disappeared into what Gretchen was sure was the master suite.

Tonight was kind of soon, but it didn't mean it was too much to ask. For the moment, Gretchen was kind of in Molly's debt. Heading down the short hall, Gretchen found her room and started to unpack. She didn't have much and quickly realized she had nothing to wear that was appropriate for her new job. Luckily the condo wasn't far from the shopping area so Gretchen wouldn't have to worry about borrowing Molly's car.

For the first time in ages it seemed, she pulled out her cell phone and quickly checked her account balance. Her cell phone had been in her pocket when Declan attacked her. It had been collecting dust in the drawer next to her bed after Claude had returned it to her, about a month into her new life.

She hadn't needed money being holed up in the mansion, so there was still a good amount there. She was no longer receiving the stipend for working at MacDonald Estate and with no other income she would have to make her meager savings last. Hopefully, she could find a good bargain. Grabbing her purse Gretchen headed for the door.

"Molly I'm going out!" she called and after a few minutes without an answer she left.

It took a few minutes, but Gretchen managed to find her way to the shopping district and find a store that sold the type of clothing she would need. It had been a few years since Gretchen had shopped in a store like this. It reminded her of her wilder days as Liz, short for her middle name Elizabeth. As Liz, Gretchen had been a total party girl. She'd been a regular at the clubs surrounding her college, and although she had never joined a sorority, she had a standing invite to all Greek events.

Those had been frivolous days, filled with a torturous beauty routine and a catalog of drinking games. At least until she'd trusted the wrong guy to get her a drink. Gretchen shook thoughts of that mistake from her head. She wasn't Liz anymore; she was Gretchen, and she was a lot wiser for it.

Scanning the sales rack, Gretchen picked out a pair of shiny black jeans and a green corset top. She then headed for the rack of scarves. Choosing a short black one she tied it around her neck. It might look a bit awkward, but it would cover her scar. Her next stop was a shoe store where she found a cute pair of black flats. Her new outfit was simple and club appropriate, but still comfortable. Now her only task was finding her way back to the condo in time to get ready for the night.

❈❈❈

"Finally," Molly whispered to herself as she flopped down on her bed. Today was the first day of her new life. An independent life. The mansion was miles away, and so was Shane. *I can finally have my peace.*

"You will have no peace."

The voice was back. Molly sat up and shook her head, trying to dispel the voice.

"You are in danger."

Molly stood and began to unpack her bags. Ignoring the voice hadn't done anything to help in the past, but at least it gave Molly a sense of sanity.

"Continue to ignore my warnings and see what happens."

Molly tensed remembering the way her body had burned only a few weeks ago.

"Forgive him." The voice was back to its old tricks.

Molly relaxed a little.

"Forgive him before everything is lost."

You seriously need a new mantra.

"Fuck," Molly cursed herself for answering back.

She waited for an answer, but none came. As quickly as it had come, the voice was gone. With Gretchen out shopping, Molly was truly alone in her apartment. She should have welcomed the feeling, but instead she felt more vulnerable than ever.

CHAPTER 9

Gretchen took one final deep breath before returning to the front of the house. All the lights, smells, and sounds were harsh on her partially trained senses. A dull headache throbbed at the base of her skull. It was times like this when she regretted forgoing extra training with Claude. Gretchen pasted a smile on her face as she pushed through the writhing bodies on the dance floor and over to the main bar.

It had only been two months since Gretchen had started working in Molly's club, but she'd taken to it surprisingly well. Although, Gretchen was sure it had a lot to do with the amazingly well trained staff. They had been very accommodating as Gretchen got a feel for her new job.

"You've got an admirer." Mack, the bartender, pushed a pink concoction towards Gretchen and pointed to down the bar.

Gretchen didn't have to look to know who it was from. She picked up the drink and headed down the bar to where Lyle sat. Lyle was currently renting a room in Molly's basement sanctuary. Ever since he'd laid eyes on Gretchen, the young Vampire had made his interest clear. He was cute, but Gretchen still wasn't interested.

"I don't drink at work." Gretchen placed the glass in front of him.

"Then what about meeting up later?" He fingered her now signature scarf.

"Whoa there Romeo, she's not interested." Molly appeared next to them.

Lyle smiled and threw an arm around Molly's shoulders.

"Come one Mol, let Gretchen answer for herself."

"I'm really not interested," Gretchen piped up quickly.

"Alright, alright, but if you ever change your mind," he said and disappeared into the crowd of people on the dance floor.

"Thanks," Gretchen said, and Molly just shook her head.

"No problem, but honestly if you had to date a Vampire. Lyle isn't a bad catch."

"He's cute, but I'm not ready to date just yet. It still hasn't been that long since we've been on our own."

"Don't tell me you still have Claude on your brain." Molly frowned.

"It's an illness," Gretchen supplied.

Molly laughed before handing Gretchen the pink concoction that was still sitting on the bar.

"As the owner, I'm telling you to drink up."

Gretchen rolled her eyes before downing it. The liquid held almost no taste, but it burned her throat all the same. She coughed and set the empty glass on the bar.

"I don't think I'll be taking up drinking again anytime soon," she gasped.

Molly patted her on the back before walking away. Gretchen followed her movement through the crowd and made a mental note of who she sat with. If Molly was spending more than a few moments with this particular group then, one or more of them had to be important.

Molly's establishment was becoming the most popular club for Vampires in the area to hang out in. She didn't exactly condone feeding on the premises, and most of the Vamps abide by her rules. They flocked from all over just to get a moment in her presence. Gretchen had overheard a few of the Vampires discussing Molly as if she were some kind of royalty. Being sired by Maura, she had some of the oldest Vampire blood running through her. Being the only female Maura ever sired made her an oddity.

Gretchen had learned a lot about Vampire society in the few weeks she'd been away from the mansion. There were pure-blooded, or born Vampires, and then there were the turned Vampires. Of the pure-blooded there were seven family lines. Each family had jurisdiction over a continent, after that point turned Vampires came into play and things got complicated. Gretchen hadn't fully sorted out the details, but to put it simply the closer your ties to the pure-blooded, the higher your status.

After finishing her third run for the night, Molly found her again.

"Enough work, come hang out for a bit," she urged dragging Gretchen over to the VIP section.

"Sometimes I wonder if you hired me to work or to be your wing girl," Gretchen said and Molly smiled.

"A little of both."

Gretchen laughed at that and turned her attention to the group of Vampires who anxiously awaited them.

Molly quickly ensconced herself with one of the male Vamps, giggling and flirting. That left Gretchen to entertain the rest of the group. It wasn't too hard, as she called upon her old persona of Liz, initiating drinking games and frivolous conversation. Luckily, none of the male Vampires in the group seemed interested in her sexually. That was another thing Gretchen had learned.

Male Vampires were all very forward about their intentions towards a woman and very possessive. Once one had staked his claim the others pretty much backed off unless the woman showed a competing preference.

Gretchen was just beginning to enjoy herself when there was a commotion by the auxiliary bar.

"Sorry boys, duty calls," she said cheerfully.

Security had already handled the scene by the time she got there. She craned her neck to see who was being escorted out by the bouncers only for a shot of fear and anger to run through her. She could have sworn that it was Declan. She pushed through the crowd, but by the time she got to the door the man was long gone.

The only other way to confirm her suspicions was to check the security cameras, but that would only be possible after her shift. If it really were Declan, she needed to know. She wanted her revenge, and if he was stupid enough to come looking for her, then she would surely get it.

✵✵✵

"Declan! At My Club!" Molly slammed her mug of blood on the counter.

Gretchen nodded and showed her the still shot she'd pulled from last night's security footage. She had wanted to show Molly sooner, but Molly had been preoccupied entertaining her guest all last night. Unlike Gretchen, Molly wasn't hesitant about exploring her dating options.

"If he comes back. I want to deal with him personally."

Molly didn't give any indication that she had heard Gretchen's demand. She just sat there muttering curses

99

for a moment.

"Sweetheart, as much as I would love to let you have your revenge. I have to notify the boys. It was part of the agreement for them staying the hell out of my business." She finally came back to reality.

Gretchen sighed and nodded. She was angry, but Molly was right. She did have to tell the boys, but that didn't mean she couldn't convince them to let her kill Declan once they were finished with him. Molly pulled out her cell phone while Gretchen thought of all the ways she could torture Declan before ending his pitiful life.

Her musings were cut short as her own cell began to ring. It was just a text, probably just one of the waitresses asking for time off, but when she opened it time froze as real life came crashing in on her. The text was from her brother.

❋❋❋

Maura sat quietly in the overstuffed chair, placed directly next to the massive brick fireplace of the cabin's living room. Axel sat on the couch nearest her with his brother Rod, while Declan chose the seat directly across from her. She raised an eyebrow at his impetuous glare. He was anxious, his foot shaking restlessly and his hands clenched together on his lap.

They had been sitting in silence for nearly ten minutes, she loved seeing him squirm with the anticipation of her next order. They were lucky she was allowing them to sit. In the old days, she would have made them stand or kneel on the hard ground, but those days were gone, and the men were so much weaker. They could not withstand her usual brand of torture and Maura knew she needed them at their physical best if she had any

100

chance of regaining what she had lost.

"I need new recruits, strong men, fighters." She finally spoke.

She watched the men's faces, not entirely surprised by their different reactions. Axel was stoic, as usual. Not because of character, but out of a lack of understanding. Rod smiled, if his smarmy grin could be called that. He had been an asset from day one, taking charge of the financial situation. In just a couple of months, he had already secured a moderate sum of money, almost enough to upgrade their living conditions. Declan, on the other hand, stiffened in his seat, his face slightly paler than usual. Maura forced herself to maintain her indifferent mask. She could enjoy Declan's unease without letting the others know.

The larger her army grew, the fewer days he had to live. He was no fool. He had failed her one too many times, and his obsession with that Gretchen girl had made him weak and unpredictable. Without her magic, she relied mostly on her weak ability as a Vampire to control the minds of these men, and his infatuation with Gretchen easily undermined her pull.

"Axel can hit up the gyms in the area, under my supervision of course," Rod offered as Maura knew he would. She flicked her wrist in his direction simultaneously agreeing and dismissing the pair.

They stood and headed for the door. Declan stood as well, but her glare rooted him in place.

"Is there more?" he asked between clenched teeth, but his eyes were to the floor.

"I need you focused on the task at hand. Not that girl. You still have some use to me otherwise I'd have killed you months ago."

He clenched his fists at her words, his eyes snapped up to meet hers. After a brief staring contest, his eyes returned to the floor.

"I still own you. Remember that." Maura smirked.

"Yes, my queen." His shoulders slumped in a defeated manner.

Now that he had been reminded of his place, Maura decided to use his distraction as part of her plan.

"As long as you remember your duties, I will allow you to hunt the girl."

He straightened, and a smile crept to his lips.

"And when I find her?" The hungry look in his eyes intrigued Maura.

"You will bring her to me, alive."

Maura stood and headed up to her room, leaving Declan to stew in his anger and resentment.

CHAPTER 10

The drive to Berry Hill had been shorter then Gretchen had expected. She felt a little like Alice in Wonderland being back in her hometown. Not that she had many fond memories of the place, but anything was better than her current reality. The town had changed a lot since she had last visited her family. The opening of a large superstore on the edge of town had left the once busy local businesses almost desolate, the only places remaining a hair salon and old Ms. Myrtle's craft shop separated by the town's small movie theater.

Where there had once been fields of berry bushes were now new housing developments. There were so many new streets it was hard to recognize the turn that would take her to the older part of town where her parents lived. It had been a few years, but she still managed to find her way. Parking behind a blue minivan she didn't recognize, she sat in her rental car slowly gaining the courage to do what she came here for. She took a good look at the house she had grown up in. It would probably be the last time she ever saw it.

There were a few subtle changes, but for the most part it was the same. The two-story home was the same shade of light green her mother had fallen in love with after watching it featured on her favorite home show. A season appropriate flag hung from its post next to the porch stairs.

Even the creepy little gnomes she had hated so much still sat in their carefully selected spots amongst her mother's prized rose bushes. The tree her family had planted when Gregory had gone off to the military was bigger now. The trunk looked sturdier and the leaves fuller. There was even a bird feeder hung from one of its thicker branches. Just like this house, her family, on the outside, looked perfect.

Molly had been surprised to find out Gretchen still had family, and had urged her to go and make her final goodbyes. The problem was, Gretchen, in some ways, had already said goodbye to them. Her relationship with her parents had been rocky since her teen years. Grace, her sister, had never forgiven her for kissing some boy she liked in high school. It was a silly grudge to hold, but that boy was now Grace's husband.

Gretchen hadn't even been invited to the wedding. Even the family dog only tolerated her. Fancy, the poodle, was a very affectionate show dog. She loved pretty much everyone but wouldn't let Gretchen so much as pat her head. The only member of the family she had a good relationship with was her brother, Gregory. It was because of him that she had relented to Molly's urging. The thought of being around her family was just as stressful as the thought of running into Maura.

"It shouldn't be so hard just to get out of the car," Gretchen groaned to herself.

She was losing her nerve, and she knew it. Her hand reached slowly for the start button on her car. No one had seen her pull up, so it wasn't too late to just leave. She dropped her hand with a curse and forced herself from the car. She'd driven all the way here, she couldn't back out now. This wouldn't be another regret on her already long list.

She marched around the house to the back yard. It was a beautiful Saturday afternoon, and she had smelled charcoal and molasses as soon as she had pulled up. Her family always liked a good backyard barbecue. At first, no one noticed her as she approached. They were all too busy laughing and joking with one another. Gretchen stopped for a moment taking in the sight.

A little boy around three was chasing Fancy around the yard. His big brown eyes glittering with youthful excitement as he awkwardly toddled after her. He had curly brown hair and freckles that made it quite clear that they were related. Her brother-in-law was at the grill with her father and Gregory. No doubt talking about sports judging by the way her father was emphatically waving his arms around. Her mother sat at the table with a heavily pregnant Grace sipping lemonade.

Gretchen was surprised at her restraint. She had been practicing for months to try and control her extra abilities and this was the ultimate test. Her emotions were running high and yet she felt normal. She wasn't inadvertently hearing people's conversations, her nose wasn't burning because of all the different smells and her eyes weren't going in and out of focus. They noticed her then, she knew because all talking had ceased and everyone was now staring at her. She smiled careful not to show teeth. Not that she had gigantic fangs or anything, but just as a precaution.

Gregory smiled at her, but no one else seemed to make a move. Her family was staring at something behind her and that's when she felt him. A warm tingle spread through her body from the base of her spine to her feminine core. Ever since she had given in to temptation her body had been hyper aware of Claude's presence. Gretchen fought the urge to run as he got closer to her and her family. They would already have questions, and she didn't want to add to them.

Gretchen's mother was the first to greet them.

"Gretchen, you should have told us you were coming," her mother said, embracing her like she actually cared. Then she turned to Claude with a knowing smile, "and you must be Felix. Gretchen has told us so much about you."

Gretchen cringed. She had never mentioned Felix to anyone but her brother. Her mother had probably heard about him from Gregory and assumed that there was more going on than what there had been. The old Gretchen would not have been above dating a professor. She looked at Claude who despite being slightly tense in posture was maintaining a neutral expression. He smiled at Gretchen's mother, and it looked almost genuine.

"Mother," Gretchen began, but stopped when Claude draped his arm over her shoulder.

"I'm Claude, the new boyfriend," he said

Gretchen felt her control slip just a little. How dare Claude tell her mother that they were dating?

Taking a deep breath, Gretchen willed her trembling fist to relax at her side. It was the first time since she had left the mansion that she had felt this worked up, but it was also Claude who was standing beside her. Claude, who had somehow managed to not only find her, but follow her to her parent's home. She forced a smile, hoping her shocked mother would mistake her furiously red face for a strong blush.

"Oh! Well, it's so nice to meet you."

Gretchen's mother blushed offering her hand for him to shake.

"It's a pleasure to meet you, as well." Claude kissed her mother's hand.

She watched in horror as her mother giggled and looped her arm in Claude's to give him a tour of the house and introduce him to the rest of the family. Grudgingly, she followed them. There was no telling what Claude might say, and as much as Gretchen hated it, there was too much at risk for her not to be on the same page now.

"Everyone, this is Gretchen's boyfriend, Claude," her mother said as they reached the patio.

Everyone greeted him nicely, except Gregory. He glared at Claude while gripping his hand tighter than necessary. Claude didn't flinch, even as the veins were bulging out from Gregory's hand in effort. It was a tense few seconds as they stared each other down. Gregory finally smiled and released his hand. Claude had passed the first test. Gretchen rolled her eyes at the blatant display, but she wouldn't expect anything less from her older brother. He had always done his best to protect her, even when she had been at her most destructive.

After the introductions, Gretchen's mom forced Claude into a seat next to her at the table. The real inquisition was about to start. Her family was being way too nice, but then again Claude was still a stranger and appearances had to be kept.

"So tell me how you two met?" Her mother asked.

Gretchen bit her lip to keep herself from ruining her mother's obvious joy. Gretchen had finally brought someone nice to meet the family.

"I saved her life," Claude said simply, and Gretchen glared at him.

"If that's what you want to call it," she mumbled, knowing that he would hear it anyway.

"Saved her life?" Gregory asked, taking more of an interest in the conversation.

Her family had known about her previous destructive behavior, but Gregory was the only one who knew what had really changed her.

"I was hiking in the woods behind MacDonald Estate when I heard a woman calling for help. I found Gretchen in a clearing. She had been bitten by a venomous snake," Claude said.

"A snake in Scotland?"

Gregory didn't look convinced.

"I know, very rare, but it was close enough to spring, and she somehow managed to aggravate it," Claude replied.

"Oh, I'm sure it wasn't that hard for Gretchen to aggravate it," Grace joined the conversation, and Gretchen frowned at her.

"She can be abrasive at times," Claude laughed.

Gretchen had expected Grace's comment, and maybe Claude's as well, but that didn't stop her blood from boiling. She wasn't sure if she was more angry or embarrassed.

"Well, it must have been an awful experience," Gretchen's mother said, and Gretchen decided it was probably safer to focus on her mother, who at the moment was being surprisingly neutral.

"You have no idea," Gretchen slipped.

She even fussed over the collar of her shirt, making sure it was still covering her scar. Her emotions were getting the better of her.

"She hated not working and having to deal with the after effects of the venom," Claude clarified for her.

He reached over and squeezed her hand gently as if to reassure her.

"I'm sure it was Felix she was more anxious to get

back to than work," Grace said.

Claude's grip tightened around Gretchen's hand.

"Really, Grace?" Gregory snapped at her.

Grace stood, signaling for her husband.

"It's so nice to see Gretchen finally settling down. She always had a tendency to bounce from guy to guy," Grace said with a smile before taking Henry's hand and walking away.

"I'm sorry. Grace's pregnancy has made her very moody," Gretchen's mother excused, and Claude nodded as if in understanding.

"My past isn't one to be proud of either, but people change. Even if others aren't willing to see that." Claude looked pointedly at Gretchen.

She pulled her hand from his and smiled at Gregory.

"We should go catch up and let Claude get to know mother and father better," she said standing. Gregory nodded and followed her into the house.

"So what's really going on here? That guy is definitely not your boyfriend, even if it's obvious you are into each other," Gregory said as soon as they were alone.

"Felix is dead," Gretchen blurted, and he frowned before pulling her into a hug.

Gretchen hadn't realized she had started crying until Gregory wiped a tear from her face.

"What happened?" he asked forcing her to look at him. It was something Gregory had always done when she had come to him like this. The familiarity of it had her sobbing more. She didn't want to give him up. She didn't want this to be the last time she saw her brother.

"His past caught up with him, and because we were close, I got dragged into it. It wasn't a snake that bit me. I was attacked and Claude saved me." She began fidgeting with her turtleneck again. Gregory noticed and grabbed her hand, pulling it and the cloth away to expose her scar.

"Fucking Hell! Is this why you disappeared?" he yelled, and Gretchen clung to him desperately.

"Shhh! Parents will hear you. I don't know if I'm really in danger or not, but I can't risk it," Gretchen pleaded through her tears.

"So who the fuck is this Claude guy?"

"He was also close to Felix. He came to the estate when he heard Felix went missing, and it was pure luck that he heard me fighting my attacker. He's been protecting me and teaching me how to protect myself."

"I don't like it. I'm not letting you handle this on your own. I didn't have a choice the last time, but this time, I can't let you run away. You are staying here. If they come after you again, we will go to the cops. Fuck it, I'll protect you," he said hugging her tightly.

Gretchen wished it were that simple. She wished that she could stay with her brother and work things out with her parents. Maybe even with Grace as well, but that couldn't be her decision. She wasn't human anymore. She forced herself from her brother's warm embrace which should have been harder than what it had been.

"You can't. I'm sorry. If someone does come looking for me here, tell them I died, disappeared, anything that means you have no contact with me." Gretchen pulled her collar back into place and wiped her eyes. Despite the sharp pain in her chest and the tightness of her lungs, she walked away.

Her feet felt heavy. Her whole body felt heavy. It was only her determination to keep her family safe that allowed her to smile when she saw her parents laughing with Claude on the porch, to keep smiling as she said goodbye and not crumble or show any sign that something was wrong.

Gretchen didn't protest when Claude guided her into the passenger seat of his car. Didn't bother asking what had happened to hers. She couldn't allow any emotion right now as her family stood on the front porch smiling and watching them leave.

"I'm truly sorry for your loss," Claude said taking her hand in his.

She snatched her hand away, staring through the window as he pulled the car into the street. Watching as her parents turned away and Gregory stood like a statue. She hadn't been able to look into his eyes during their final goodbye, and now it was too late. Her older brother, her rock, was gone forever.

CHAPTER 11

Claude had no idea what had come over him. Gretchen had made it very clear the night she left that she wanted nothing further from him. That was something Claude had tried for the past few months to accept. He shouldn't have even had to try. Gretchen should have been out of his system after their first intimate encounter, but if anything, it had only made him want more.

She had managed to wiggle her way into his dead, rotten heart. A heart that many would say he never had to begin with. Claude rubbed his chest where his heart should be, at times he wondered if he had one, but today had been proof enough that he did.

He had been on his way home from meeting with the blood supplier when he had seen her driving through town. He had only meant to follow her long enough to find out where she was staying. It would put his mind at ease and since she was staying with Molly it would put Shane at ease to know as well. Then she had turned onto the road leading out of town and he'd been afraid she was making a run for it. The last thing he expected was the long drive to what turned out to be Gretchen's family home.

Cat's parents died when she was in college and Molly

had been a foster child. They had nothing to lose when they were turned. In all of this time, Claude hadn't thought about Gretchen having a family. People who would miss her and whom she would miss as well. Claude gave himself a mental kick. He could hurt for her, but that wouldn't stop her from hurting. Staring at her wasn't going to help either, so he turned his attention back to the road.

He had no idea how to comfort her as she sat silently in the seat next to him. His one attempt had been quickly brushed off, and he couldn't exactly blame her. He'd heard everything that had been said between her and her brother. Felt the waves of despair pouring from her even as she did her best to hide it. The silence was killing him so he turned on the radio. Switching through the stations he flicked glances at her to see if she responded to any of the choices, but she didn't. He didn't really care for modern music so he finally settled on a jazz station.

The woman beside him was not the woman he had come to know. His Gretchen had been strong and independent, quick to put Claude in his place. Her eyes had always been full of fire and determination. Now she looked so pale and fragile, curled into the fetal position in the sleek, black leather seats of his sports car. Her mood was so dreary that despite using the heater Claude still felt a chill.

Her eyes were dead as they stared out the window, unfocused and unmoving. She was merely a shell and it was entirely his fault. Somewhere along the drive she had fallen asleep and not knowing where she was now living he had no choice, but to bring her back to the mansion. Claude hoped everyone would still be sleeping when he got there with Gretchen, but no such luck.

"What happened?" Xander greeted them at the door.

"She just needs to rest." Claude shifted Gretchen's weight in his arms. He pushed passed Alexander and took Gretchen to her old room.

He carefully placed her on the bed and tucked the covers around her body. It was all he could do not to lay on the bed next to her, to hold her in his arms as she slept. Instead, he placed a gentle kiss on her forehead.

"Everything will be okay," he whispered before leaving the room.

He so desperately wanted to stay with her, but he knew he couldn't. The most he could do was make sure she was cared for until she was well enough to leave again. Gretchen would leave again, and this time Claude wouldn't fight. It was the least he could do for her.

❈❈❈

"Is she okay?" Cat asked as soon as Claude joined them for breakfast.

"I don't know. She went to say goodbye to her family," he said staring blankly at his mug.

Cat wasn't used to seeing Claude so morose. That was more Shane's thing.

"She had family?" Xander looked to Cat for confirmation.

This was news to Cat as well. Even though she had been the closest to Gretchen, it had never occurred to her to ask if she had a family. They had mostly talked about Cat and Xander's wedding and Vampire lore.

"I never asked. She was pretty closed off about herself," Cat said with a shrug. She took a sip from her mug and studied Claude further.

There was a sense of defeat about him that scared

her. It was similar to the funk Shane had been in when they had all thought Molly was dead. This definitely didn't bode well for The Shadows matchmaking plans.

"I'm okay," Claude said meeting her eyes.

"You are not okay. Gretchen is obviously not okay," Cat began, but stopped herself. Being harsh wasn't the best way to go about things. "Just don't give up on her. She needs you now more than ever."

There was a flicker of hope in Claude's eyes, but it was fleeting.

"I'm the last thing she needs." Claude left the table.

"Right now isn't the time to play matchmaker," Xander scolded Cat.

"Like that stopped Claude playing matchmaker for us. It sucks that Gretchen had to sever ties with her family, but you know what that means? We are her family now, and we have to take care of her no matter what. They are destined to be together just like we were, and they will get over this. Even if I have to lock them in a room for a couple years."

Xander rolled his eyes at her. "Let's just focus on getting Gretchen functioning first," he replied, "also, call Molly and let her know what's going on."

"Yes, sir!" Cat saluted him with her middle finger before going to make the call.

❋❋❋

Molly checked her watch again. It was getting late and Gretchen was still nowhere to be found. She couldn't blame the girl for wanting to spend a bit more time with her family, but Molly hadn't pegged her for the irresponsible type. Gretchen would have called by now. Molly dug in her purse for her phone. It was normally stored in the convenient side pocket, but the last time she'd been using it she'd tossed it in a hurry.

Molly smiled to herself as she recalled Brody's eagerness to please. Despite bringing a different Vampire home almost every night, Molly had a strict no penetration rule that included biting. She found that was an easy way to avoid the dreaded mating issue. Molly belonged to no one, but herself. She wasn't going to give any arrogant young Vamp the opportunity to claim otherwise.

Her hand finally clasped the slim metal case around her phone when it began to vibrate. "It's about time." Molly let out a sigh of relief, only to frown when she realized it was Cat and not Gretchen calling.

"Why the hell haven't you been answering your phone?" Cat's annoyed voice screeched from the speakers.

"I'm a busy girl. What is it?" Molly was actually glad to hear from her friend, but she hadn't appreciated Cat's tone.

"Gretchen is here at the mansion. We will be keeping her for a few days. She didn't take well to saying goodbye."

Molly sighed and shifted the phone to her other ear. "I'm sure she will be fine here with me. I'll come get her tonight."

"Mol, I know you two desperately want your independence, but right now it is better if Gretchen stays here. I promise this isn't some matchmaking scheme for her and Claude. You can come see for yourself, but I can't let you take her right now."

Molly desperately wanted to protest, but Cat had always been the protective type. If she said Gretchen was in bad shape, there was no reason for Molly to question it. However, there was one variable that just didn't add up. "Wait, how did she even get to the mansion?”

“Come by tonight, and I’ll explain everything.” Cat didn’t wait for Molly’s reply she just hung up.

Molly glared at her phone for a moment before tossing it back in her bag. The club could go without a manager for tonight, but Molly had to see what she was dealing with. If Gretchen was going to be out longer than a week, she would be forced to find a replacement.

✿✿✿

“Are you feeling better?” Cat stood in the open doorway of Gretchen’s room.

Gretchen sat up and sighed heavily. “I’m fine.”

Cat frowned at her and entered the room, taking a seat on the edge of Gretchen’s bed. The woman pulled Gretchen into a big hug. Gretchen wished it made her feel better, but she was completely numb. It was a feeling she hadn’t felt since she first woke up as a Vampire.

“You are not fine. I’m so sorry things turned out for you this way. I know how it feels to be turned without your knowledge, but I didn’t have as much tying me to the human world as you did. I feel like such a bad friend for not even asking about it.” Cat brushed at a tear that had fallen from her almond shaped eyes.

Gretchen was suddenly angry. Her heart beat furiously in her chest, and she felt heat rising in her cheeks. She threw back the blanket that was covering her and jumped out of the bed. “I need to get out of here.” She was down the stairs in a minute and almost made it to the front door when she was blocked by a solid wall of male Vampire.

“I’m leaving,” she ground out, but it was to no avail. Xander stood his ground glaring down at her as if she had lost her mind.

"Not just yet. I can't in good conscience let you leave in your present state."

"My present state?" She repeated incredulously.

Xander snorted and pointed to the giant mirror hanging on the wall behind her. "No offense, but at the moment you are worse off than Shane."

Gretchen spun around to face her reflection and what she saw gave her more than a little pause. Her curly hair tangled and slightly matted, listed to one side, her face was almost ashen, and her eyes were red and puffy from the hours of crying she had done. She also realized she wasn't wearing any clothing. Suddenly feeling the cool air against her bare skin, her hands came up to cover her breasts. Her whole body blushed, and she ran back up the stairs.

Cat was waiting with a robe in her hands and a smug smile on her face.

"Take all the time you need. It's been pretty lonely being the only girl in the house again." She closed the door behind her as she left.

Gretchen could hear Cat's muffled laughter as her footsteps moved away towards the stairs.

CHAPTER 12

Gretchen pulled the covers tight around her shivering frame. Her room was too cold or rather she was too cold. The mansion was usually kept at a nice 70 degrees Fahrenheit, so it had to be her. After her freak out, no one else had bothered to check on her. In fact, the whole mansion had been dead silent, not even her advanced hearing had been able to detect much more than a little movement around the grand abode. She didn't know what she hated more, the fact that she hadn't been able to remain aloof in this situation or the fact that everyone was tiptoeing around her.

She closed her eyes and listened again, this time picking up on the sound of someone showering nearby. Judging by the closeness of it, it had to be Claude. An image of his naked body flashed through her mind, and she gasped as warmth spread across her body and concentrated at her core. Thankful for the brief respite, she conjured up his image again. Imagining him standing under the spray of his shower, water cascading over his shoulders and down his back, veering inward at the V just above his firm muscular backside.

Gretchen tossed the covers away from her and slid her hand down her now overheated body to her aching wet center. She rolled her clit with her thumb as her pointer and middle finger delved inside her. She stroked herself until she was thrashing about on the verge of climax, but it just wouldn't come. She needed more. Without thinking, she got out of bed and marched over to Claude's room. She pushed open his door and marched straight for the bathroom.

Claude met her half way, still naked and partially wet. She pounced on him. Their lips met in a hungry kiss, tongues dueling as he turned to press her against the wall. No words passed between them as he positioned his engorged flesh at her entrance and pushed in, stretching her, filling her. Gretchen wrapped her legs tight around his waist, and he drove into her with wild abandon. His hips slamming into hers, her back burning with the friction of their movements against the wall, but she didn't care. She needed this. She needed to feel, something, anything, everything.

❉❉❉

Claude was surely going to hell, but for this moment with Gretchen, it was all worth it. The feel of her hot and wet surrounding him, her muscles tightening and releasing, stroking him into oblivion. He was in his own personal heaven. He'd spent the entire day outside of the mansion, trying to give her the space she needed, but when he'd heard her come into his room, all thoughts of chivalry died instantly.

His need for her was too great. Her legs gripped him tighter around his waist, forcing him to change his pace and rhythm. Instead of punishing thrusts, he was pressed deep inside of her, the tip of him brushing the furthest reaches of her depths.

Her hips settled into a slow grind as her eyes locked with his. The raw look of passion in those gray orbs was nearly his undoing. They watched each other as her movements brought them both over the edge. Her inner muscles clamped down on him like a vice before her whole body shook in orgasm.

He could no longer restrain the inevitable and gave himself over to his own release. Fully spent, but not quite flaccid he continued to slide in and out of her until her body relaxed, and she slumped forward. Her breathing shallow and even, she had fallen asleep.

Careful not to wake her, Claude tightened his grip around her waist and moved away from the wall. He carried her over to his bed and placed her under the covers. He went to the bathroom and wet a washcloth before returning to where she lay and gently ran the cloth over her body. She stirred slightly as he washed her female parts. She had been very tight, indicating that he had been her first in a long while. It made his chest swell with pride and a little bit of possessiveness. He moved the washcloth away only for her hand to grab his.

"More," she whispered.

Gretchen was awake, her eyes still full of passion and yearning. A small smile tugged his lips as he tossed the washcloth aside.

"More of what?" The predatory growl of his voice wasn't something he was used to, but the way her body flushed in response made him forget to ponder the significance of it.

She reached up and cupped his face before brazenly guiding his head down to where his hand had just been.

"More pleasure!" Her words came out in a deep moan as Claude wasted no time giving her what she wanted.

If her mouth tasted like sour apple, her arousal was the caramel sauce. She was sweet and musky, and he didn't even mind tasting himself there. In fact, it made it even better, knowing that he had left his mark. Her hands fisted in his hair tugging and pulling him closer as her hips bucked against his mouth. He swirled his tongue around her clit, delighting in her sharp intake of breath.

He suckled her, and her knees pressed into his temples as her body shook with impending orgasm. He'd never wanted anything as badly as he now wanted to taste her cum mixed with her blood. He used his tongue to mimic the movements of his dick in her vagina and as soon as he felt the first spasm of her orgasm he sank his teeth into the flesh around her clit. Her fluids flooded his mouth as he greedily took all she had to offer. Claude was completely unprepared for his body's reaction to the heady mix.

Like an instant jolt of sexual energy, he became overwhelmed with the need to claim her. He slowly withdrew his fangs and moved up her body. Impaling her on his raging hard on. He rode her even more frantic than before, and he sank his teeth into her shoulder right where it met the curve of her neck. He drank from her and fucked her with a drive that scared him. He was going on pure instinct, and it wouldn't be satisfied until she was his in every way.

❋❋❋

Gretchen smiled to herself as she woke up tucked against Claude's hard muscled body. His soft snores tickling the back of her neck. Last night had been beyond description, and her body was definitely paying for the strenuous affair. She reached up to touch the place where Claude had bit her. Her skin was smooth and without flaw which made her feel a lot better.

When he'd initially struck, she'd frozen in panic, but

there hadn't been any pain, only intense pleasure that had made sex an all new experience for her. He'd bit her many places last night, but when he'd bit her there, it was like a revelation. Something shifted inside of her and made all the bad go away, nothing else in the world mattered except the two of them and the joining of their bodies.

No wonder Molly only brought other Vampires home. Vampire sex is fucking awesome!

"Good morning, beautiful." Claude's sleepy voice interrupted her mental 'Yes!' dance.

He placed a gentle kiss on her cheek, then her ear, and finally directly on the spot he had bit her shoulder. She shivered as arousal shot through her. She turned to face him. His hard member pressed against her belly. His hazel eyes were filled with emotion, with love, and it tugged at her heartstrings.

I should never have done this.

"About last night." She started to get out of bed, but he grabbed her waist, holding her captive in his arms.

"Don't." There was a somber look in his eyes.

She opened her mouth again, but instead of allowing her to speak he kissed her. It wasn't as rough as their previous kisses, but soft and gentle and full of unspoken promise. A promise of love and forever and Gretchen caved. She would surrender if only for this moment. If the last few days had shown her anything, it was that reality sucked and although she knew she had to return soon. For now, at least, she could believe in fairy tales.

CHAPTER 13

Declan smiled to himself as he scrolled through Gretchen's old social site. Trying to find the bitch the old fashioned way hadn't got him anywhere, but this was already showing some promise. The girl on the site was a far cry from the uptight, mousy woman he had known. Pictures of her as a blondie with straight hair scrolled across the screen. Most showed her with a drink in hand, smiling with other females with the same bleached and straightened style. California girls, you've got to love them.

Her last post had been some time before she had arrived in Scotland, but there was enough information left to discern the perfect way to get his revenge. The only male consistently featured on her site was actually her brother. He clicked on a link bringing him to the brother's site.

Jackpot! The man still lived in their home town, luckily not too far from here.

He patted his pockets and cursed.

"Excuse me, I'm sorry to ask, but I forgot my cell at home. Mind if I borrow yours for minute?" he asked the young girl next to him.

At least having to use the public computers at the local library had been good for one thing. Declan wouldn't have to wait until he was back at the cabin to make his call. Maura would be pissed that he'd forgotten his leash, but he hoped his new plan would ease the punishment he was sure to get.

The girl seemed shy but eventually nodded and carefully pushed her phone towards him. She eyed him anxiously as he picked it up and dialed the number listed on the brother's site. The brother answered on the first ring.

"Hello," a gruff male voice answered.

Declan smiled and cleared his throat. Remember be polite, no need to ruffle his feathers...yet.

"Is this Gregory Jones, brother of Gretchen Jones?"

The man on the other line sighed heavily into the phone, his breath coming across the receiver as static.

"Yeah, who's asking?"

Great, he didn't immediately hang up.

"My name is Declan Murray. I worked with your sister on the MacDonald Estate. She has been absent for quite a while now. Has she contacted you or her family lately?"

"No, why do you ask?" There was an edge to her brother's voice.

I guess old Gretch didn't contact her family after all. Stupid Bitch. This was almost too easy.

"Oh, well, she left in kind of a rush so as a friend I thought it would be nice to bring her the things she left behind at her place? I'd have shipped them, but there were a few things I didn't trust sending by mail. Is there any possibility we could meet up?"

There was a pause on the other end, as if the man were pondering the suggestion.

Come on, come on, just say yes!

Declan fought the urge to drum his fingers on the table in anticipation and frustration. The girl from whom he had borrowed the phone was staring at him intently. No need to arouse any suspicion from her or anyone else around them for that matter.

"Where and when?"

Finally, any longer and I might have lost my cool.

They finalized the details before Declan ended the call. He sat there reveling in satisfaction until the girl next to him tapped his shoulder.

"Excuse me sir, can I have my phone back now?" A hint of annoyance in her voice that undermined the shy hunch in her posture.

Declan smiled at the girl and handed her back her phone. He closed out his session on the computer and headed for the door. Nothing could get to him today. In a week's time, Gretchen would be at his mercy once again.

❅❅❅

Gregory went online and searched Declan Murray as soon as he'd given his name. He knew a few things from Gretchen's perspective, but it never hurt to get a deeper understanding of a possible threat. Declan Murray didn't have much of an online presence and the few articles that did pop up weren't much help. He'd taken over for Dr. Aiken after his disappearance and was a member of some treasure hunters club, not a very popular one either judging by a few less than friendly comments on his profile. Not exactly the kind of guy who inspired loyalty or gained a following.

He was a pissant, certainly not the main threat, but Gregory was going to take this opportunity to get to the bottom of it. This Murray character had to be involved in whatever trouble Gretchen had found herself in. He would meet with him, beat the truth out of him, and then, if needed, turn the whole situation over to the authorities.

He didn't even mind that the kid wanted to meet out in the woods. It was better for Gregory to placate his violent streak without having to worry about witnesses calling the cops. If Gregory could solve this problem then Gretchen could come home for good. That way he could make sure she managed to stay out of trouble for once in her life.

He dug around in his desk to find the card Gretchen's friend had given him in case someone had contacted the family regarding her. Flipping the card in his fingers for a moment, Gregory decided to skip making that call. Claude Morgan didn't look like he could fight worth a damn, but he had enough strength at least for Gregory to feel comfortable letting him take care of his sister. He could handle this himself and would give the guy a call when he settled things with that Declan character. No need to get his sister all worried over nothing. He stuffed the card in his wallet and went back to work.

❈❈❈

Two days of orgasmic bliss and Gretchen was ready to forget about her bid for independence. Watching Claude as he slept, he looked like the angel she had first thought he was. She traced his mouth with her finger, remembering the many ways he'd used it to bring her pleasure and not just the sexual kind. Claude was smart and funny and well, for lack of a better term, perfect.

In between sex they had talked about their favorite books, the direction they saw the economy heading, even a little about all the traveling he'd done before the guys settled at the mansion. This man was a part of history, and she was seriously considering him as her future.

"Keep staring at me like that and we won't make it to breakfast." Claude shifted position pinning her under his body. He wiggled his eyebrows at her, and she laughed.

"Can't you just feed me?" Gretchen leaned over and licked him where he liked to drink from her.

He hissed and his hips pressed into her. He was aroused and she wasn't in the mind to say no to a quickie. She reached down and guided him inside of her. Opening her legs wide so he could bury himself in deep. Without waiting for him to respond, she sank her teeth into him. Warm fresh blood filled her mouth as he filled her with his seed. Her own body fell into orgasmic bliss as she fed from him. She didn't want it to end, but he finally pulled her away.

"I won't be alive much longer if you take anymore," He hissed falling to his side. He was a little paler than usual, and Gretchen instantly felt guilty.

"Sorry, I've never drank from anyone before."

He looked at her, and a possessive look settled onto his face.

"You won't be drinking from anyone, but me," he growled pulling her into him he kissed her hard. Her body reacting instantly to his touch.

She had never been this horny in her life, but a soft knock on the door broke the sexual fog she was in.

"Everyone is waiting on you two." Shane's voice called through the door.

"Be right out," Gretchen called.

She kissed Claude one last time before getting out of bed. She threw on his oversized robe and waited for Claude to put on his pajama bottoms. There was no use getting dressed when they would only be discarded once breakfast was over.

They held hands as they entered the kitchen. All eyes were on them both curious and a little disgusted. Gretchen was surprised to see Molly was there also.

"You look sickeningly chipper for someone who's supposed to be having a breakdown," Molly said giving her a hug.

It was unexpected, but not unwelcome. She'd gotten closer to Molly in the last few months, but neither woman had ever been the affectionate type.

"I have an excellent physical therapist," Gretchen whispered.

She knew the others could hear it well enough, but old habits die hard. Xander nearly spit out his sip of blood and Claude pulled Gretchen into his lap a proud look on his face.

Cat studied them for a moment before grinning like a lunatic.

"You're mated!" She jumped up from her chair and began to do a happy dance.

Xander raised an eyebrow at his wife before chuckling and shaking his head. "It's about time you settled down."

"I don't see why it's such a big deal. We just had sex. Lots of amazing sex, but still just sex." Gretchen felt Claude still beneath her and she turned to look at his face.

Cat stopped doing her happy dance and stormed around the table.

"You claimed her without telling her!" Cat pointed a finger in Claude's face. Her jovial grin was now an angry snarl.

Xander moved quickly, putting himself between his wife and Claude as she yelled countless obscenities at him.

"Claimed me? What does that mean?" Gretchen moved away from Claude, feeling the need to put some distance between them. It was the only way she'd be able to think straight.

Claude sighed and hung his head. He pinched the bridge of his nose before turning a pleading look on her. "When a male and a female Vampire share blood during sex it bonds them together. It's like a wedding of sorts. You carry my presence with you in a deeper way now than even my bond to you as your sire. When you asked—I thought you knew."

"You thought I knew!" Gretchen was horrified. He had tricked her, and now she was—she didn't even want to think about it.

"You really are an ass," Molly said and pulled Gretchen away from him.

Gretchen was so furious she didn't even look back as Molly dragged her out to her waiting car.

"I can't believe this." Gretchen was crying now. Reality had reared its ugly head, and there was no place to escape.

CHAPTER 14

Claude smiled wanly at the desperate woman in front of him as she rubbed her body against his. Claude hated clubs, but they were the perfect hunting ground for Maura. Not just Maura, but other Vampires as well. Of course, they had cleared out as soon as he had made an appearance.

Other Vamps in the area weren't exactly fond of anyone sired by Maura. Not that he could blame them. In the old days, as Maura's man slave, he'd been ordered to destroy any Vampire he came across. Killing one's own kind was as much as a black mark on him as having Maura's blood in his veins.

"You want to get out of here," the woman purred, bringing Claude's attention back to her.

Claude took a good look at the woman for the first time since she'd sidled up to him on the dance floor. She was pretty and willing, his only requirements for a sexual partner. Before Gretchen, he probably would have said yes immediately. After Gretchen, the woman's over-done makeup and glitter covered clothes were a complete turn off.

"Maybe another time," Claude said, though he didn't mean it.

The woman huffed and stormed away from him towards the bar. She obviously wasn't used to being rejected. With her gone, Claude did another walk around the club, but there was nothing of concern at this particular venue. Claude checked his watch and saw the night was only half way over. Either Maura was hunting elsewhere or her new minions were smart enough not to stalk the clubs until closer to closing time.

From what Claude remembered of Declan, it was probably the latter. Declan wasn't particularly bad looking, but his personality was enough to turn any woman away, even the desperate and drunk ones. The ratio of men to women in the club began to shift into the red zone, so Claude decided to try one more place before calling tonight's hunt a bust.

He took a deep breath as he exited, clearing his nostrils of the pungent cocktail of sweat, perfume, and alcohol. He'd take the long way to the next club before putting his nose through that torment again. He probably should have started there first, seeing that the first and only sighting of Declan had been at this particular venue.

"Are you stalking me now?" A familiar voice said when he entered.

Claude frowned before turning to Molly.

"No, I'm hunting."

She raised an eyebrow at him, her arms crossed over her chest.

"I thought you were strictly into bagged blood? Well, I guess if anyone broke the mold you would be the one."

"Hunting Maura. What are you doing here?"

"This is my club. How do you think I was able to afford to leave so quickly?"

That was an interesting bit of news. Cat had mentioned that Molly owned a business, but hadn't given any more detail than that. He should have figured that Molly hadn't just been enjoying a night on the town when she'd spotted Declan.

"What about Gretchen?" His curiosity got the better of him. He was trying his best to give her space, but it was a harder task after mating her.

"Don't worry about her. Just leave, if I see any sign of Maura I'll call."

Of course, Molly wasn't willing to share with him. There was no love lost between the two of them. Even before Molly's death they had been somewhat at odds. Now, after last month's screw up, both Molly and Cat had circled their wagons around Gretchen as if he were a real danger to her.

"Fine, but be sure to call. I know you think you're all badass now, but trust me when I say Maura is a lot more than you could handle on your own."

"I'm not an idiot, now get out of my club before I have security throw you out."

Claude left and headed to a nearby bar. The only two dance halls had been a bust, but the town dive bar might be a better hunting ground than expected. A few blocks from Molly's club he caught an all too familiar scent coming from a dark alley, death. He poked his head around the corner using his excellent vision to make sure he wasn't walking into a trap. Satisfied that it was clear he made his way into the alley.

The smell got stronger as he approached a group of dumpsters, the smell mixing with that of rotten food. The smell of death was strongest at the trash bins, but there was no hint of blood, not even a drop. Taking another look up and down the alley he cursed before lifting himself up to look into the dumpster. Under a thin layer of raw garbage lay the pale exsanguinated bodies of three women. Maura! Anger and fear sliced through him as he took in their familiar features. All three women had brown curly hair and light freckling on their cheeks.

❈❈❈

Gregory stepped out of the car and eyed the cabin in front of him. It was larger than he had thought it would be. Hell, it was almost a lodge with two stories and a wraparound porch. It looked straight out of a magazine, dark green shutters and all. Greg felt around his back, his hand going to his pistol. He was sure he wouldn't need it, but he brought it just case. It was time for some answers.

He marched up the stairs and knocked on the door. There was no answer, so he knocked again. He checked his watch, and it was the time they had agreed to meet. Maybe the kid had thought better of his plan. Greg was just about to leave when the door swung open. Instead of the man he was expecting, stood an older woman. She was gorgeous with her long flowing black hair and pouty red lips. The only thing that gave away her age were the soft wrinkles around her eyes and mouth. Greg's dick jumped in his pants as she eyed him and licked her lips.

"Sorry Ma'am, I think I got the wrong cabin." Gregory nodded at the woman, but her smile faded into a scowl at his words.

"Did you just call me Ma'am?" Her voice dropped to a deadly low tone.

Sensing that something wasn't quite right with this situation Greg began to edge his way back down the stairs only to encounter a solid wall of muscle at his back. He turned to see the biggest SOB he'd ever encountered glaring down at him. Not one to be intimidated, Greg puffed up his chest and glared back.

The man grinned revealing a pair of long sharp fangs and Gregory realized he'd made a mistake. He was out of his depth here, and he should have called for help. He dug in his pocket and hit the speed dial he'd programmed in for that Claude guy. It was a lost cause, but maybe he could at least keep his sister out of harm's way.

❈❈❈

Claude had just finished destroying yet another punching bag when the buzz of his phone got his attention. He didn't recognize the number and almost didn't answer, but this niggling feeling that it might be important forced him to press the call, button.

"Hello," he barked, but on the other end there was only rustling, followed by a male scream and silence.

Claude listened more, and his blood ran cold as he recognized the sound of blood gurgling in a windpipe and an all too familiar cackle.

"Take Mr. Jones inside, he will do fine in my new army." Maura's voice came through the speaker.

"I'm glad you are pleased," a male voice said.

"You did well, Declan, for once, but you still have to bring me the girl." Maura's voice was farther away this time and almost inaudible.

There was silence for a while, but the call hadn't disconnected. Claude ran to Shane's room and burst in, not bothering to knock.

"What the hell?" Shane said sweeping what was no doubt a plethora of illegal drugs away from sight. Claude would talk to him about that later, but for now they had bigger problems. Putting his phone on mute Claude demanded Shane's help.

"I need you to trace this call. It could lead us to Maura's hideout."

135

Upon hearing that Shane jumped into action, rushing to his computer he began typing away. Claude continued to listen in while he worked. There was a loud thump, and a new voice came across the speaker.

"Hey Axe, be gentle with the guy. He's our new brother." The voice was nasally and grated on Claude's nerves.

"Sorry, Rod." A deeper voice.

"And check his pockets. He doesn't seem like the type to come empty handed."

"Yes, Rod."

More shuffling.

"Holy shit! Give me that. I'll handle the gun you keep checking his pockets."

A brief pause with more rustling.

"Oh, and if you find a phone smash it."

The rustling was getting louder, which meant they were getting closer.

"Shit, we're almost out of time." Claude wanted to maintain an element of surprise. It was the safest way to approach Maura, so he hung up.

"What the hell, man. I was so close!" Shane jumped up from his seat and glared at Claude.

The man's temper was running high, and Claude could understand. They all had reasons to want the location of Maura's hideout.

"Did you at least get a good search area?" Claude ran a hand through his hair in frustration.

Shane typed a little more on his keyboard. "Yeah, there are only two cell towers where the call could have originated from. If we focus our patrols to this mountain area, it will take us about a week to find her."

"A week! Shit." Claude began to pace.

"It would have been easier if it were in the city, but she's in the mountains. She could be in a cabin, underground, or even in a fucking tree house." Shane had joined in on Claude's pacing.

"Fuck it. Give me a map. I'm taking first patrol. You let Xander know what's going on." Claude snatched the map from Shane's hand and headed for the door.

Maura had Gretchen's brother, and there was no way he was going to let her keep him.

CHAPTER 15

Claude studied the map spread out across the desk in the study. For the past two days, they had systematically combed the area but had come up with nothing. His hands shook violently as he attempted to mark off the area he had just patrolled. Xander crossed the room and snatched the pen from his hand, marking it for him.

"You need to calm down." Xander squared off with him.

Claude glared at his close friend and shook his head.

"Would you be calm in my shoes?" He was so enraged. Spittle flew from his mouth as he spoke.

Xander wiped a drop from his face, flinging it away in disgust.

"If you want to save him, this has to be done right. Take a walk, beat the shit out of something, but don't go on patrol in your condition. You will only end up dead and no help to anyone." Xander's harsh words pierced the red haze of his brain and Claude's shoulders slumped in defeat.

He fell back onto the sofa and covered his face with his hands.

"Gretchen can't know. She hates me already, but I will have no chance if she finds out about this. I love her so much I can't lose her like this. I can't lose her to Maura." A single tear broke the flood gates of his emotions, and he began to sob. Not caring about his ego he accepted Xander's embrace.

"Am I interrupting something?" Cat glided into the room as if she didn't know that a closed door meant a need for privacy.

Claude pulled away from Xander and quickly wiped at his face.

"Claude needed a good punch in the gut is all," Xander said with a smirk and pulled his wife into his arms.

Claude turned away, he couldn't watch them together. It was too hard. Instead, he walked over to the window and stared out into the night. The sun was beginning to rise, and it stung his eyes, but for once he welcomed the pain. It was a mild distraction from his own inner turmoil. After a few moments, Claude realized the couple had forgotten he was there. He slipped out of the room to give them privacy. Instead of going to his room, he headed for Shane's.

"To what do I owe this pleasure?" Shane didn't bother hiding his stash this time.

"I need you to find an easier way to track Maura. Our plan now will take too long and may even give her a heads up to our arrival."

Shane sighed and moved over to his computer. He began typing away, but stopped when Claude moved to look over his shoulder.

"I can't work with you breathing down my neck."

"I'm surprised you can function with all the poison you've been putting in your system."

Shane glared at him, and Claude glared back before leaving. With Xander occupied, and Shane being anti-social, Claude decided he should take Xander's advice and find something to beat up.

❄❄❄

Cat paced in the kitchen with her phone in her hand. She had to tell Gretchen what she had overheard. That Maura had her brother. Xander hadn't realized she had overheard, and it was hard not to yell at him for being so cruel. What if Gretchen found out in the worst of ways?

"She mustn't know."

Cat didn't even jump at the now familiar voice. The Shadow appeared on the other side of the kitchen.

"I have to tell her." Cat began to dial Gretchen's number, but a sharp pain shot through her hand causing her to drop the phone.

"She will die and all will be lost."

Cat didn't bother picking up the phone again. Maybe she shouldn't be so trusting of this shadow. It had set Molly on fire and now was causing her pain, keeping her from doing what Cat felt deep down was the right thing to do.

"Don't you ever come with good news?" Cat massaged her now aching hand.

"Just be thankful for my help and heed my warning. The time is near, and your cooperation is key." The Shadow disappeared, and the pain in Cat's hand immediately subsided.

"Well, that was interesting." Cat jumped as Shane appeared from the shadows.

"Seriously Shane! Stop being such a creeper!"

"I'm not the one talking to ghosts," he replied getting a mug from the cabinet.

"If you saw it too then I'm not as insane as you think."

He stopped what he was doing and smirked at her.

"Not exactly a comeback. Cat, my dear, you are losing your bite."

"This from a man who looks like the grim reaper. Molly loved you for your vibrant, outgoing personality. You need an intervention and a prayer if you are going to have any chance with her again." She didn't wait for his reaction, she just turned and stormed out. Once this whole Claude and Gretchen thing was settled, Shane would be in for a rude awakening.

❋❋❋

The Shadow looked down at the man resting peacefully before her. He resembled his sister with his brown hair and pale skin, but that was where the similarities ended. His face was harsher with a strong brow ridge and jutting chin. His angular face matched the deep cut of his muscled torso.

He was strong, a warrior. Even now his spirit warred with Maura's dark hold over him. It was with all her strength that The Shadow slowed his change. Keeping him safe from Maura in the only way she could and buying time for him to be found.

She placed a shadowed hand on his cheek, and to her surprise, her hand took shape. Not the shadow she was used to in this plane of existence, but her old hand, flesh and blood, rested upon his cheek. He stirs, turning into her touch, and she smiles. He knows she's there. Her excitement fades as the sound of feet approaching means she must leave. It wouldn't be wise if she were discovered. I'll keep you safe, I promise. The Shadow fades away just as Maura enters the room.

❋❋❋

Maura admired her latest recruit as he lay tied to the

141

dining room table. His brown hair was cut short, but there was enough length to hint at bountiful curls once it grew longer. He was fair of skin, but his hands were rough, most likely from the same work that toned his muscular body.

This one was a warrior. She had seen it in the way he conducted himself in the brief fight with Axel. It was only by a chance blow that Axel had overpowered him. It had been two days, and he still hadn't woken. A testament not only to his amount of fight, but also to the weakness of her blood.

Even with regular feeding she was still getting weaker. She could feel it in the stiffness of her joints and the creak in her bones. Her skin may be almost flawless, but her inner workings were aging faster every day.

"You wanted to see me." Rodney approached her cautiously.

He was a good asset but had recently gotten too cocky. Even suggesting she might take him to bed instead of Axel. He'd been unprepared for her idea of amusement, and now he tiptoed around the house. She turned to him and smiled, putting him even more off kilter.

"I've waited long enough. Tell Declan that it's time."

"Yes, my queen." Rodney scurried away like the rat he was.

She turned back to Gregory and placed a kiss on his lips. Her heart beat rapidly at the thought of him at her mercy. He would fight her, and she would break him, just as she had all the others before him. The only thing she would spare him would be watching his sister die by her hand. It would be better if he believed it were the traitors. He only needed to wake up.

CHAPTER 16

The club was crowded, even for a Saturday night. Mostly humans, which Gretchen appreciated. Ever since she'd come back, the other Vampires had started to treat her differently. The male Vampires acted as if they were afraid to get close to her. The female Vampires glared and whispered, like she was the unpopular kid in high school. She knew the reason; it was all because of Claude.

He had marked her. She was his Vampire bride, and as such, became just as much a pariah as he was. She reeked of him. Not even a thousand showers could get his smell from her skin. She loved it and hated it. Just as she loved and hated him. There was no denying that in just a few days he'd managed to weasel his way into her heart.

Gretchen pushed her way through the crowd and over to the back bar. She'd only just reached it when the hairs on the back of her neck stood up. She turned around coming face to face with her biggest nightmare.

"Declan!"

"The one and only, did you miss me?" His smug smile filled her with dread.

Where was all the fight she'd saved up for this very moment. Her trauma was getting the better of her.

"You have a lot of nerve showing up here." Gretchen fought the urge to signal security. This was her fight, no need to involve anyone else.

"I just wanted to have a chat. I have a new friend who is dying to see you," he laughed, but the sound was lost in the pulsing dance beat filling the club.

Gretchen raised an eyebrow at him before she slapped him with all her strength. His body jerked with the impact, and he whirled on her quick. Grabbing her shoulders, he shook her violently. Suddenly he was pulled away, and Gretchen was being shielded by club security. He screamed an address at her as he was being dragged away. She caught most of it before the rest was drowned out by the music.

"Are you okay?" Ben, the head of security asked. He was a Vampire. He knew what Declan was.

"I'm fine." Gretchen couldn't meet his gaze. Her eyes fell to her shoes, and she noticed a card on the floor. She picked it up and froze in place. Tears forming in her eyes, she fell to her knees.

Ben quickly picked her up and ushered her into the staff area. He asked her questions, but she couldn't hear them for the rush of blood in her ears and her loud sobs. Clutching her brother's driver's license in her hands, she began to pray. Not for strength or guidance, but for vengeance and death. Without a doubt, Declan's actions demanded retaliation and retribution. She would kill Declan for sure.

❀❀❀

"I'm not letting you go," Molly said blocking the door. For such a small woman, she had quite a grip. Even for a Vampire.

She was glad to see Gretchen was no longer sobbing

hysterically, but this was no better. Upon getting the word from Ben, Molly had rushed to the club and shut it down for the night. Gretchen had sobbed all the way back to the condo.

"That bitch has my brother!" Gretchen pushed at her again. She was crazed, a Vampire on a mission, but Molly could not let her go to her death.

"And if you go alone, she will kill you and still have him." Her fingers dug into the door frame cracking the wood deeper.

Molly sighed with relief as Gretchen seemed to back off. If she'd gripped the frame any harder, it would have to be replaced. She waited a moment before dropping her arms.

"I just hate that he's mixed up in this," Gretchen said before bolting out the door. She was gone before Molly could stop her.

Fucking Bitch! Claude is going to kill me if anything happens to her.

Molly picked up her phone and texted Cat. At least she knew the address so maybe the guys could beat her to Maura's lair. She wasn't surprised to see Cat calling almost as soon as the text went through.

"How in the world did this happen!"

"Stupid bitch bolted. I told her it wasn't a good idea to go alone, but she knows they have her brother. I told you it was a stupid idea to keep that from her. Are the guys on their way yet?"

"Claude was out patrolling. He will probably get there first, but Xander and Shane just left. It wasn't my call to keep it a secret. Anyway it's too late now."

Molly could hear the regret in her friend's voice. Not saying that Gretchen knowing sooner would have helped the situation, but at least Molly wouldn't feel so guilty about keeping it from her the past few days.

"Fuck it. I'm going. Are you coming?"

"Xander's going to kill me, but hell yeah. We need to support our friend." Cat ended the call first, and Molly ran to her room to change. There was no way she was wearing a mini skirt and heels to the mountains.

❋❋❋

Gretchen tossed the cab driver a twenty and got out. The sweet old man rolled down his window as she rounded the car.

"You sure you don't want me to wait?" He cast an uneasy glance at the dark road. Gretchen had asked him to drop her off at the base of the trail. The car noise would give away her approach to the cabin.

She pasted on a smile and waved him off. "Have a goodnight."

She didn't wait to see him pull off as she began to jog down the wide path. As soon as she heard him drive away she picked up her speed. Determined to get there and meet Declan head on. She would die before allowing her brother to become one of Maura's Men.

Gretchen's train of thought died as soon as she saw Declan standing in the middle of the clearing ahead, he was headed toward the dark cabin that loomed ahead. Her vision turned red, and her arms began to swing automatically in a haphazard frenzy. All the training she had received over the past few months didn't bother to surface as a burning lust for vengeance settled into place.

❋❋❋

Claude crouched low in the brush as he studied the cabin in front of him. There were no lights to be seen from the window, but Declan sat in the shadows

146

of the porch. The Vampire could easily have detected Claude's arrival if he were using his Vampire senses, but he obviously wasn't or didn't care. His gaze was trained down the path, waiting for Gretchen no doubt.

Claude's heart beat faster in his chest at the thought of her coming here. It was a blatant trap, but she wouldn't care with her brother's life at stake. As if his thoughts had conjured her, Gretchen appeared down the trail a bit, running full speed towards Declan. Claude had no time to react as she crashed into the other man, arms flinging wildly as she attempted to hit him.

If she weren't in real danger, Claude would find the situation amusing. Declan easily deflected the majority of her hits with timely side steps, but he wasn't always quick enough. She connected a few times with great affect, sending the man sprawling to the ground. Pride swelled in his chest as he watched her face her real life demon.

It wasn't until another figure appeared behind her that he made his presence known. Jumping from his hiding place in the bushes, he attacked the wall of muscle. A punch to the gut, the side, and the jaw did nothing to move this mountain of Vampire.

"Silly man." The mountain laughed before easily lifting Claude off his feet.

Claude struggled, all too familiar with this particular choke hold.

"Bring him to me." Claude froze as Maura appeared a few feet away. The mountain started to move towards her and Claude really began to panic.

Where are Xander and Shane when I need them!

Claude swiveled his head as much as he could, searching for Gretchen, but she was nowhere to be found. He was only slightly relieved to see Declan's lifeless form still on the ground. At least that much of a victory had been won. The giant's grip tightened on Claude's throat restricting his air flow even more.

Black spots began to crowd out his vision, and his head began to swim. If he survived this, he would have a few very choice words for Xander and Shane about the timeliness of battle.

✼✼✼

Declan was dead. His blood pooling around his lifeless body and soaking into her pants. She was relieved and mortified and about to be sick. She bolted to the nearest bush and hurled, hand shaking as she wiped her mouth. She almost forgot the other half of the battle until she heard Claude's scream.

She whipped around in time to see Claude crumple to the ground at the feet of Maura. That was the only person this woman could be. She was beautiful other than the evil grin on her face. Her eyes boring holes in Claude as he fell and cried out in agony.

Without thinking Gretchen charged. She took the woman off guard managing to knock her to the ground before she was pulled away by the giant at her side. Her adrenaline pumping, she fought off the guy and rushed to Claude's side. He was still and unconscious as she cradled him.

"Wake Up! Claude, please. I need you! I love you!" She was hysteric.

"He's dead child, and soon you will be too." Maura raised her hand high above Gretchen's head.

Gretchen shielded Claude's body from the coming blow, but it never came. Instead, a bright white light surrounded them, and she could hear Maura cackling away. When the light faded Gretchen and Claude were alone in the clearing in front of the cabin. She searched

148

the area and spotted Molly at the edge of the clearing. Her skin held a light glow, and her chest heaved as if she had just run a marathon. Cat soon joined her a shocked expression as she stared at her best friend.

❈❈❈

Xander and Shane ran towards the clearing where Claude was going head-to-head with Maura and her new henchmen. Shane split off and headed into the cabin but was waylaid by the scrawniest of the two men. That left Xander with the larger of the two. He shook out his shoulders before charging straight ahead. It had been a while since he'd had a good hand to hand.

Claude seemed to be struggling with Maura but there was nothing Xander could do to help him in the moment. Out of the corner of his eye he saw Claude fall to the ground, just before the male he was fighting caught him with a right hook to the chin.

An all too familiar cackle rang out into the night, turning his blood to ice. Xander stumbled back, blinding light clouding his vision. He didn't believe he had been hit that hard, the light must be emanating from somewhere else. By the time the light faded and he was able to regain his bearings, Maura and her two henchmen were gone.

How had they disappeared so fast?

Xander had no idea. They had taken off before the light had subsided. It had provided the cover they needed to slip away without a trace. He was confused. Maura had the upper hand; he'd seen Claude fall. He searched the clearing with relief as he saw that Shane was just a few feet away.

"We should check on Claude." Shane said.

Xander looked at the gaunt man beside him and

149

nodded. Shane was lucky the man he was fighting was no stronger than a flea. Otherwise, Xander would have been alone in facing Maura and her henchmen. They rushed over to Gretchen who sat sobbing over Claude's still form. There were no visible marks on him, but Xander knew Maura's power allowed her to kill in other ways. He tried to pull Gretchen up, but she fought him off, desperately clinging to Claude.

"Give them a moment." Cat came up beside him. He glared at his wife and cursed.

"How? Why?" He was so angry he barely managed to get the words out.

"I couldn't sit at home alone and worry. I had to be here not only for you, but for Gretchen." Cat hugged him close, his anger melting away with her embrace. The threat of Maura was still out there, but at least for now they were safe.

Molly and Shane emerged from the cabin with Gretchen's brother. He hadn't even noticed Shane had slipped away in his moment of anger. The two supported the man on their shoulders. The man was unconscious and in no better shape than Claude, but Xander could sense Maura's blood in his veins. He prayed the man hadn't suffered too many unspeakable horrors in his short time with that demon wench.

CHAPTER 17

"Declan, dead, deadweight! My plans, my plans are ruined. They will pay, they will all pay! That bitch may have escaped my curse, but Claude didn't. He'll be dead soon, and then it will time for the rest of them. I won't just sit idly this time. RUN! That is your great plan? Maura does not run!"

Rodney watched Maura as she paced the small hotel room angrily rambling the same incoherent nonsense she'd started two days ago. Whatever she had been in the middle of doing back at the clearing had completely robbed her of her beauty.

Her once flawless skin now marred with age spots, sagging with wrinkles, and dare he even say jowls. Her long ebony hair was now brittle and white, falling in a ragged mess over her frail hunched frame. She was not the woman who had enticed him and his brother. The altercation had weakened not just her body, but her mind. Her eyes flitted wildly around the room even as she spoke directly to him. It was time to bail. This ship was sinking fast, and he had no intentions of ending up like that bastard Declan.

It would be so easy just to knock her out and takeoff, but just as he was about to reach for the nearby table lamp, Axel arrived with Maura's meal. The poor girl barely made it into the room before Maura pounced.

Like a starving wild animal she demolished the poor girl's throat, blood spattering everywhere, ensuring the need to move on by cleaning time tomorrow. At least the girl didn't scream. Her body struggled initially before slumping over lifeless.

Glassy spaced out eyes stared back at Rodney, and he had to look away. Maura had held him and his brother in some trance, but now it had weakened enough for Rodney at least to feel some kind of remorse for her prey.

When Maura finally let the body fall her skin and hair had regained some of its youthfulness, but not enough. She was still grotesque; even Axel cringed a little as she reached for him. Still he went to her, and Rodney shook his head before leaving the room. There was no way Rodney could stomach what was about to happen. His brother had it the worst at the moment, but her hold over him was stronger.

The longer they stayed, the harder it would be to get away. Even starved and crazed she was regaining her power every time she fed, and it wouldn't be long before she regained enough of her faculties to put Rodney back in her thrall. If it weren't for Axel, Rodney would have already taken all the money and made a run for it. He loved his brother, but sometimes he was a major burden. He had to handle the situation delicately if he were going to get himself and his brother out alive.

❋❋❋

Molly frowned as she surveyed her half empty club. News of Maura lurking in the area had severely deterred the Vampire community in the area. Even Brody had distanced himself from her. She wanted to be pissed, but she couldn't exactly blame them. Maura was a real piece of work and would surely be back to retaliate for Molly interrupting her curse. Molly hadn't even realized what she was doing until it had happened. She'd come stumbling into the clearing just as Maura was casting her spell over Gretchen and Claude.

There'd been a force field surrounding the pair and Molly had just reacted. Using her mind she'd latched on to Gretchen and somehow managed to shield her from whatever horrors Maura had in store for her. For all her efforts, all Molly got in return was two days of exhaustion and the complexion of a glow worm. The light had since dimmed, but was still enough to have people giving her a double take.

At least Gretchen had been safe, and Molly had been able to locate her stud of a brother. If Shane hadn't been present Molly probably would have stood gawking for a good hour before thinking to untie him. Now that he was awake maybe she should do the neighborly thing and bring him a pie. Molly laughed out loud at the very inappropriate turn her thoughts had taken. She may be reckless, but she wasn't stupid.

Molly made her way over to the bar to check on things. With Gretchen taking care of her brother and Claude, she was out of a manager indefinitely. Still she held out hope that Gretchen would return soon, so instead of hiring a replacement, Molly was taking a more hands on approach to her business.

"Cheer up, Boss. Just give it a few weeks and the blood suckers will be back." Mack, the bartender, set a glass of red wine in front of her.

He was human, but he knew a lot about the Vampire world. Molly had never asked how or why, but today, it helped to have someone equally on the outside to commiserate with.

"I'm not worried about them."

"News on the red says there's going to be an official investigation by the Trues."

Molly rolled her eyes at Mack's quirky slang for the Vampire gossip network and the pure-blood Vampires. "As long as they don't put a ban on my business, they can do whatever the hell they want."

Mack leaned over the bar, getting real close to her. "I might have to take a vacation if they come."

Her eyes widened as she stared at Mack intently. She could read nothing other than human about him, and given that he was cool about Vampires, he probably wasn't a hunter. She decided to let the man have his secrets.

"Fine just make sure you call in first. I don't want to be short a bartender and manager." Molly downed the rest of her drink and stalked off. She needed a vacation herself.

❊❊❊

The mansion had been a somber place since the fight. With Claude still unconscious and Maura still on the loose. Breakfast was more a time to plan than the family affair it had been just a few days before. Gregory had thankfully awoken shortly after arriving at the mansion, but hadn't been thrilled about being a Vampire. He mostly stayed locked in his room only opening the door for Gretchen.

"Any luck tracking Maura?" Xander eyed Shane expectantly.

Shane sighed and shook his head. "Nothing."

He took a sip of his breakfast. It was already beginning to cool and congeal. He pushed his mug away and focused on the stacks of documents they managed to

154

retrieve from Maura's lair.

"Any idea what that light could have been?"

Cat choked on her breakfast at Xander's question. Sputtering and gasping for breath, tiny drops of blood sprinkled the counter in front of her. Xander patted her back as she gained her composure.

"Seems like you have something to share." Shane took a moment to study Cat.

Ever since the fight she had been acting a little strange. She was wary of Molly when she came to visit, and Shane had caught them arguing a few times, but they'd both go silent as soon as he came near. Something was up with those two, but he would let it go for now.

"I should go check on Gretchen. She gets so caught up taking care of Claude and her brother, sometimes she forgets to eat." Cat stood, but Shane raised a hand to stop her.

"No, I'll go. I need to chat with her anyway. She is the only person, other than Claude, who knows what happened before we arrived." He was out of his seat and down the hall before she could protest.

Shane shook his head when he found Gretchen curled up next to Claude. He'd known it was only a matter of time before those two found the common ground of love between them. It was too bad Claude wasn't able to enjoy it at the moment. He closed the door quietly and shuffled back to his room.

He paused as he passed Molly's empty room. She had insisted on staying at her condo, but she came to visit every night. They had worked well together the night of the fight. She hadn't minded his touch as they'd helped Gretchen's brother from his restraints. She had even smiled at him when they had returned safely to the mansion. It made his heart swell, and a smile graced his lips. Maybe there was some hope for them yet.

✹✹✹

Naked and exhausted Claude lay on a bed of needles. The only comfort in his living hell.

Bright! So Bright! Endless...

Claude's self-defeating thoughts were cut short by the now familiar roar of his demon pursuer. Claude forced himself up onto his feet, the sharp gravel cutting into his skin with every move he made. The bed disappeared as if it were never there at all. Claude couldn't be certain if he only dreamt that it appeared at all.

He kept his eyes shut for a moment longer, the only respite from the glaring white light all around him. From where it came he had no idea, but it was everywhere in this torturous maze. The sound of heavy hooves crunching on gravel forced Claude to start moving.

He cracked his eyes open wincing at the immediate sting of light glinting off gravel like polished glass. It was painful but not as harsh as looking ahead and into the direct rays of whatever blinding light source was there.

Claude lurched forward his limbs weak and achy from countless hours of avoiding his tormentor. He stayed close to the bushy wall of the maze careful not to let his skin touch the deceptive feather soft foliage.

A muted green, it had felt wonderful to lean on, but Claude had learned his lesson quickly that everything here was meant to injure. After a few moments of rest, his skin had begun to tingle and then burn. Those soft shrubs were poisonous, just a brief minute of contact, and he'd lost half of his strength.

Claude kept moving, turn after turn, dead end after dead end. The hooves got closer and the roar louder, more menacing. There was no place to hide. The jagged ground tore open his skin and left a marked trail of blood wherever he went. His only safe bet was to keep moving.

The beast would stalk him until Claude could move no further and then Claude knew it would be his death. If only he could get out of this maze, but the maze was alive. Changing and adjusting to his every move. This place was to be his grave. The grave Maura had prepared for him.

CHAPTER 18

Gregory lay huddled under the blankets of his borrowed bed. He was hiding like a coward from his new reality. He didn't want to believe what Gretchen had told him, but he had no choice. There was no other explanation for what was going on with him. Well, except that maybe he had lost his ever loving mind. Right now, the only thing keeping him sane was his solitude.

He didn't want to meet the others, even if he could now hear them as they made their way around the house among other things. Gregory had heard a lot he hadn't intended on hearing lately and light of any kind against his overly sensitive eyes had him screaming in agony. He'd thought having sand in the eyes sucked, but this, this was a million times worse.

"You will get used to it," a female voice said from outside his blanket shield.

Gregory tensed as he knew the door to his room had been firmly shut and locked. There was no way anyone should have gotten into the room without him knowing. He slowly lowered the covers, and for once in the last two days, his eyes weren't immediate balls of fire. Another shocker, the woman standing at the foot of his bed was beautiful. Not in the same way as the crazy lady that'd attacked him, but that didn't stop his male appendage from reacting to the sight of her.

She had long brunette hair that stopped just shy of her hips, a small heart-shaped face that sat upon a slim regal neck. She was small and in today's standards a little on the heavy side, but to Gregory she was picture perfect. She had curves in all the right places. It was the innocence that radiated from her that made him feel like a lecher. The blush that crept to her cheeks had him looking away.

"Who are you?"

"That isn't relevant. I just came to ease your transition. Maura will be coming after you again." The woman moved around the bed and reached out to him.

Instinctively he pulled away, but when her hand settled on his cheek, he felt instantly at ease. He could feel things shifting in his psyche as all sorts of new information became available to him. Even with everything else that was going on the warmth of her hand against his cheek felt a lot more intimate than it should. Gregory's thoughts turned to a sexual nature as he pictured her hand trailing down his cheek to his chest and even lower still until she grabbed his—the woman gasped and pulled her hand away.

"I'm sorry," he began and reached for her, but she disappeared into thin air.

Startled, Gregory jumped out of bed. Gretchen hadn't mentioned anything about ghosts.

❋❋❋

Claude fought back the panic rising in his chest as he stumbled and fell. His legs had given out and for the first time he was getting a full glimpse of his pursuer.

159

First to round the corner was a massive pair of horns, nearly six foot long. Their sharp conical tips swooped down and then up again, as if to ensure maximum damage when used as a weapon, and Claude was sure that is what they were used as.

Next came the real monstrosity. The face of a bull, torso of a man, and legs of a Shetland pony. Mottled shades of red and gray fur sprouting haphazardly across its form. The creature roared at the sight of Claude, who was now frozen in fear on the ground.

The creature came closer, snot glistening and dripping from its snout it bared razor sharp teeth. Claude instinctively began to crawl backwards, adrenaline numbing the sharp cuts to his arms and legs. The demon lowered his horns and positioned his body to charge. It hoofed the ground kicking up gravel and dust.

This is the end.

Claude closed his eyes unwilling to see death coming. Sweat poured down his forehead as he waited.

"Claude!" An angelic voice pierced the air around him.

Claude's heart sang as he recognized Gretchen's voice. His eyes flew open in time to see his last chance at survival. The beast was startled by the voice and had turned away from Claude. Giving him mere seconds to make an escape.

"Claude!" There it was again to his left. The poisonous bushes parted before him, and he ran toward the sound of Gretchen's pleading. A small part of him knew this was probably another sick joke, but his heart wanted to believe that Gretchen had somehow managed to find him and was here to help him get out.

❋❋❋

It was the chill that woke her. She'd felt safe and warm curled up next to Claude, but a sudden chill had jerked her from her rest. Claude lay completely still beside her his lips blue and his skin, cold as ice to the touch.

"Claude!" Gretchen felt for a pulse, a heartbeat, breathing, anything, but there was nothing.

"Claude!" She tried CPR, rescue breathing everything she had ever learned about how to revive someone, but he was gone. Her love was lost.

She collapsed, sobbing onto his chest as the others filtered into the room. Cat and Xander first then Shane. Cat turned away upon seeing the body, hiding her face in Xander's chest, she cried. It was Shane who approached the bed first.

He slipped an arm around Gretchen and was just about to pull her away when Claude sat up gasping for air. His arms instantly came around Gretchen holding her close as life returned to him.

"I'm here, Gretchen. I'm back." Claude refused to let her go, and Gretchen clung to him tightly. Relief washed over her as she realized the worst hadn't happened.

Cat marched across the room and slapped Claude, tears still falling down her eyes.

"Don't you ever do that again, or I'll make sure you won't be back for long," Cat threatened half-heartedly before storming from the room.

"Good to have you back," Xander called over his shoulder before pushing Shane out the door as well.

"I thought I had lost you," Gretchen sobbed.

Claude forced her to look at him. "I almost gave up, but you saved me."

"I love you," she blurted.

"I know." Claude smiled and kissed her.

161

Gretchen couldn't find it in her to get mad at him so instead she just kissed him back.

"Never leave me," she whispered as they lay in post-coital bliss.

"I think that should be my line," Claude laughed, pulling her tighter against him.

"Just promise."

Claude pulled her on top of him so that they were face to face. "I, Claude Marion Morgan, do solemnly swear to love, honor, and cherish one Gretchen Elizabeth Jones for the rest of my life."

"Your middle name is Marion?"

Claude groaned. "It's a perfectly good name."

"For a girl," Gretchen teased.

"We both know I am no girl."

"Can I call you Mary?"

"No," Claude growled and pinned her under him.

He looked genuinely upset about the idea, and Gretchen found it ridiculously cute. They still had so much to learn about each other, but they had eternity to do it.

More From Stella Williams

Paranormal Romance & Urban Fantasy

<u>Maura's Men Trilogy</u>

Xander's Claim
Claude's Conquest
Shane's Redemption

<u>Secret of Ceres Series</u>

Ferocious
Dauntless
Earnest
Zenith

<u>Langsmith Shifter Shorts</u>

Coy Wolf
A Night Divine
Bird of Prey

<u>Bloodlines</u>

His Soul to Keep

Contemporary Romance

<u>Paramour Novellas</u>

Felling Bechet
Unforgettable Valentine

About the Author

Stella Williams is a USA Today Bestselling Paranormal Romance Author, who lives in Washington State. She has a degree in Anthropology from The University of California, Santa Cruz. Stella prides herself in using her studies to create diverse worlds and characters for her novels.

You can find more about Stella on her website
www.serpentinecreative.com